Miyu Shinohara

Karen Ko

a Kanzaki   Goushi Asougi

Sword Art: Online Alternative

Gun Gale Online

IV

3rd Squad Jam: Betrayers' Choice

Keiichi Sigsawa

ILLUSTRATION BY
Kouhaku Kuroboshi

SUPERVISED BY
Reki Kawahara

CONTENTS

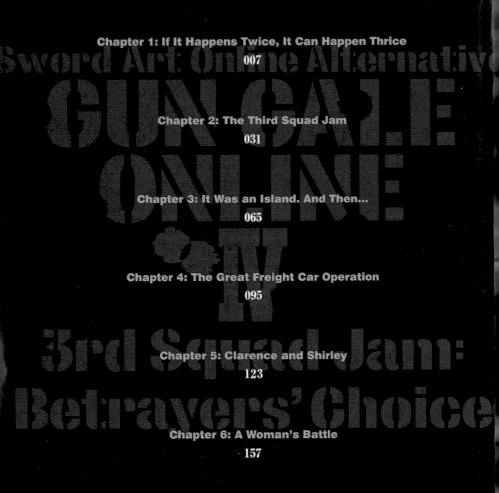

DESIGN: BEE-PEE

Sword Art Online Alternative

GUN GALE ONLINE IV

3rd Squad Jam: Betrayers' Choice

Keiichi Sigsawa

ILLUSTRATION BY
Kouhaku Kuroboshi

SUPERVISED BY
Reki Kawahara

YEN ON

NEW YORK

SWORD ART ONLINE Alternative Gun Gale Online, Vol. 4
KEIICHI SIGSAWA

Translation by Stephen Paul
Cover art by Kouhaku Kuroboshi

SWORD ART ONLINE Alternative Gun Gale Online Vol. IV
©KEIICHI SIGSAWA / REKI KAWAHARA 2016
First published in Japan in 2016 by KADOKAWA CORPORATION, Tokyo.
English translation rights arranged with KADOKAWA CORPORATION, Tokyo, through TUTTLE-MORI AGENCY, INC., Tokyo.

English translation © 2019 by Yen Press, LLC

Yen On
150 West 30th Street, 19th Floor
New York, NY 10001

Visit us at yenpress.com
facebook.com/yenpress
twitter.com/yenpress
yenpress.tumblr.com
instagram.com/yenpress

First Yen On Edition: July 2019

Yen On is an imprint of Yen Press, LLC.
The Yen On name and logo are trademarks of Yen Press, LLC.

Library of Congress Cataloging-in-Publication Data
Names: Sigsawa, Keiichi, 1972– author. | Kuroboshi, Kouhaku, illustrator. | Kawahara, Reki, supervisor. | Paul, Stephen (Translator), translator.
Title: Third Squad Jam : betrayers' choice / Keiichi Sigsawa ; illustration by Kouhaku Kuroboshi ; supervised by Reki Kawahara ; translation by Stephen Paul.
Description: First Yen On edition. | New York, NY : Yen On, 2019. | Series: Sword art online alternative gun gale online ; Volume 4
Identifiers: LCCN 2019019388 | ISBN 9781975353865 (pbk.)
Subjects: CYAC: Fantasy games—Fiction. | Virtual reality—Fiction. | Role playing—Fiction.
Classification: LCC PZ7.1.S537 Th 2019 | DDC [Fic]—dc23
LC record available at https://lccn.loc.gov/2019019388

ISBNs: 978-1-9753-5386-5 (paperback)
978-1-9753-5392-6 (ebook)

10 9 8 7 6 5 4 3 2 1

LSC-C

Printed in the United States of America

THE 3rd SQUAD JAM
FIELD MAP

N

AREA 1

AREA 2

AREA 6
[UNKNOWN]

AREA 5

AREA 4

AREA 3

AREA 1 : City

AREA 2 : Forest

AREA 3 : Wasteland

AREA 4 : Switchyard

AREA 5 : Hill

AREA 6 : Unknown

PROLOGUE

PROLOGUE

Sunday, July 5th, 2026, at 12:15 PM

"Hyaaa!"

Llenn shrieked as she ran.

A little shrimp of a girl, no more than five feet tall, with pink combat fatigues, a pink ammo pouch on either leg, pink hat, and pink gun—she was running for her life with tears in her eyes, screaming "I'm gonna die, I'm gonna die, I'm gonna die! I'm dying! Dying! Dying! Eeeek, I'm dead!" She ran at a dead sprint. Her speed was astonishing.

Pitohui's utterly unconcerned voice came through a communication device into her left ear. "Oh, you're fine! Smaller body means smaller target."

"Yes. And if it should come to it, I'll collect your bones to bury back home, Llenn!" came Fukaziroh's equally nonchalant voice.

"Hang in there," said M's voice, as calm and collected as ever.

"Ugh…"

Even faster than Llenn's sprinting speed were the bullets that tore through the air overhead. All around her, red bullet lines that indicated the path of incoming shots wove and wandered like searchlights.

"If I die because of this, I'm gonna curse you! I'll come back as a ghost and haunt you!" she screamed at her distant teammates.

But her two female comrades didn't care.

"If you die in a game, can you really come back as a ghost?"

"I think I'm skeptical on that one, Pito. But Llenn's such a good student, she might just figure out a way to do it."

They couldn't have cared one iota for the fate of the one under a withering hail of gunfire, running for all she was worth to avoid getting shot.

"You're terrible! I'll curse you whether I die or not! If you weren't on my team, I'd shoot you right on the spot!" Llenn swore as she ran—to keep from dying, to keep from getting shot, to keep surviving.

The moment she had finally cleared the reach of the bullet lines aiming at her from over her left shoulder, a new bullet came whizzing past from the right farther ahead, grazing her helmet.

"Aieeeee!"

The people in the bar watching could see exactly what a predicament the little pink girl was in.

"Oof, that's rough."

"Think she's gonna die?"

Displayed on the screen was a massive railway facility.

Over a vast stretch of concrete and gravel, there were many, even dozens of sets of railroad tracks laid out in parallel. Far too many to count, in fact.

Scattered along the tracks were a variety of stationary train cars. Some held shipping containers, some carried tanks, some carried metal boxes. Some of the cars were properly connected, and some just sat alone. A few had even gone off the tracks and rested upturned on the ground.

This place was commonly known as a switchyard, a place where many sets of tracks were used to sort out incoming freight trains.

And in this huge area, with no place to hide except behind the train cars themselves, the little pink shrimp was running for her life. All alone.

All the dozens of people watching the live feed in the bar knew her. Llenn was the champion of the first Squad Jam event and the runner-up of the second. She was known for being a difficult target, small in size with tremendous agility.

But even then, if surrounded by enemy teams shooting from all directions in a wide-open area, even she was going to get trapped and hit sooner or later.

"There's a limit to how much you can run…"

On the screen, a signal flare soared into the air. The shining-red round leaped high into the dull-gray sky, then descended lightly on a parachute.

"Oh, there's another one!"

That's going to bring more of the surrounding teams in, the viewers in the bar knew.

The flare was a signal to other teams that said *Found Llenn and Pitohui's team—help us corner them!*

They'd already shot a number of them up, and each time it happened, more squads gathered in the area. One of the many monitors hanging from the ceiling of the bar displayed a team in reddish-brown camo laying down an endless carpet of assault rifle bullets at Llenn.

There were at least three hundred yards between them and the fleeing pink rabbit across the tracks, but they fired anyway, unconcerned with ammo stock or anything else.

"Damn them! They teamed up again!"

"These people never learn…but on the other hand, it might actually work this time."

Llenn ran and ran on-screen. She didn't have time to fire the P90 in her hands. If she did anything but run, a bullet would surely hit her.

This was the virtual reality online game *Gun Gale Online*, known as *GGO*.

The third installment of the team battle-royale tournament Squad Jam, or SJ3 was underway.

Only fifteen minutes had passed since its start.

And the heavy favorites were already in major trouble.

As she ran, Llenn screamed, "I knew I shouldn't have entered!"

But it was too late.

CHAPTER 1   SECT.1

If It Happens Twice, It Can Happen Thrice

CHAPTER 1
If It Happens Twice, It Can Happen Thrice

Saturday, June 6th, 2026, at 2:20 PM

A light rain had been falling on Tokyo since the morning, and the temperature was high, making it exceedingly muggy indeed.

"Ahhh."

Karen Kohiruimaki was lounging.

"Ooooh."

All six feet of her, extremely tall for a twenty-year-old Japanese woman in college, was clad in pale-yellow pajamas as she lounged atop the low bed in her apartment bedroom.

"Ohhh."

The dull light from the rain clouds passed through the white lace curtains into her room, which was cooled and dehumidified by her air conditioner.

"Dahhh."

Like a bored bear lounging in a zoo, the owner of the room surveyed her cream-colored rug, simple furnishings, neatly organized bookshelf, clothes rack, and the P90 air gun hanging from it.

Tired of rolling from side to side in her spacious bed, Karen finally stretched her limbs all the way out and gazed up at the ceiling, grinning. "Ahhh, an afternoon with nothing to do... This is the best...," she said to no one in particular.

It was the greatest of luxuries—not doing anything, not sleeping, just lounging comfortably atop her bed while her mind wandered.

Her short hair was unkempt, her face bare—and perhaps even unwashed all day. She was really making the most of her rainy Saturday afternoon.

Next to the bed was an AmuSphere.

When the large silver goggle-like device was hooked up to a computer and placed over her head, it would take her to a virtual world where all the senses were directly stimulated in a way indistinguishable from reality.

But Karen's AmuSphere had a tiny layer of dust on its surface, a sign that it hadn't been used for some time. She hadn't played a VR game in over a month—meaning, specifically, she hadn't played the one game she actually had an account for: *Gun Gale Online.*

GGO had an individually sponsored team battle-royale event known as Squad Jam, which was typically referred to by the abbreviation SJ. There had been two Squad Jams so far, and Llenn took part in both.

The first SJ, from which she emerged victorious following battle after battle, had taken place on February 1st.

The second SJ, which she'd entered for the purpose of defeating Pitohui, and finished in second place, followed two months later, April 4th.

After that, she finally got the chance to meet Elza Kanzaki, Pitohui's real-life identity, had a horrible time, and swore that she would *never* meet her offline again. That was April 19th.

But only three times after that had she actually dived into *GGO.*

The first time was Saturday, April 25th. She sold the entire submachine gun set she'd won for being an SJ2 runner-up and used the money to buy a new P90. Her teammate, Miyu Shinohara, who went by Fukaziroh online, had already returned to her favorite game, *ALfheim Online (ALO)*, and given Llenn full control over her rewards.

"Prize? Do whatever you want! Sell them off! Just keep Rightony and Leftania in the locker where they belong, okay?"

She had plenty of money but no item, and it was quite an ordeal to find one. She must have searched through just about every gun shop in Glocken, the capital city of the *GGO* world.

The second time she logged in was May 5th, the last day of the Golden Week holiday period.

With her new P90, dyed pink once again, she met up with Pitohui to go monster hunting. P-chan the Third acquitted itself very well. The familiar contour of the grip. The light, compact body, which fit her petite size. The fifty-round magazines, which could be shot at a rate of nine hundred rounds per minute. Llenn had decided she would use this gun for the rest of her life. She would never cheat on it.

Her third login was the day after that.

She'd had some free time in the evening and decided to dive in. She was enjoying a cup of tea at a place with a nice view when she was unluckily spotted by other players. She decided to run rather than get into a big fight. If there was one thing she was good at, it was running.

Since then, Karen hadn't dived into *GGO* at all.

There were three reasons for that.

One, a new term had started at school, so she was busy with classes. In other words, she was preoccupied with real-life concerns. The game was just a hobby, something she did to pass the time. Karen was a hardworking student, and she wasn't going to let her grades slip over a game.

Two, because she had so fully plunged into SJ2 in order to beat Pitohui and allowed herself to go as wild as her instincts wanted, she actually felt quite fulfilled with what she'd accomplished during the last tournament.

And lastly, Pitohui could hardly play anymore. She turned out to be, shockingly enough, the ultra-famous singer-songwriter Elza Kanzaki, of whom both Karen and Miyu were major fans.

She had upcoming shows—a seven-city tour across the country from mid-June to early July, spanning Hokkaido in the north all the way to Kyushu in the south. That was obviously a big deal to her, so she was probably just swamped with rehearsals and practice. Pitohui hadn't logged into *GGO* at all.

If her number one partner wasn't playing, then Karen didn't feel a particularly pressing need to, either. She drifted away from *GGO*.

There were some other players she knew who were her rivals in the game and thus did not mingle with her in *GGO*, but they were very good friends in real life. These people were from the gymnastics team of the high school attached to Karen's college.

"We're super-busy these days, too! No *GGO* for now!" texted the team leader, Saki Nitobe. "But everyone's doing great! We don't have any new team members this year! It's kind of rough! But there are lots of people who switch clubs once things settle down, so I'm not giving up hope! When things ease up, we'd love to hang out and eat snacks again!"

It was very easy to see how Saki's senior year was going.

"She's really living up her youth," Karen remarked to herself idly.

As usual, she had no friends at school and was always alone, but that didn't bother her anymore. She didn't need to force herself to make friends. She could just take things at her own pace. It would all work out.

Ironically, her reason for starting *GGO* was to become another version of herself in VR, gain confidence, be more assertive, and maybe make some friends. And the conclusion she arrived at was the polar opposite of that.

"Uuuh."

She was fully enjoying her lazy afternoon, when…*bzzzrt.*

"Uh?"

Her smartphone buzzed on the shelf attached to her bed's headboard. It was her notification for an e-mail or text message.

"Urgh?"

She reached out, making full use of her long arms to grasp the phone behind her head and bring it in front of her face, being careful not to drop it.

There were seven and a half billion people living on the planet, and very few of them ever had reason to contact Karen. The one more likely than anyone else was her older sister, who lived on an upper floor in the very same high-rise apartment building.

She would send all kinds of messages. For example, sometimes she'd text Karen when she knew her husband would be home late so that she and her daughter could fill the extra seat at the dinner table. Other times it was *Let's go shopping at the department store by the train station.* Or *Mom and Dad sent some sweet potatoes and corn from home, so come and get some.* Or *How is school going?* And so on.

But because her sister was taking on the watchdog role, Karen actually didn't talk to her own parents that much.

Even less frequent was correspondance from her friend Miyu back in Hokkaido. She would bring stories about screwing up at the driving school she was attending now or about how much she was doing in *ALO*, her favorite game. Miyu was a college student, too, but she never had anything to say about classes and grades.

After that came Saki. And then M's real-life identity, Goushi Asougi, who only contacted her on rare occasions.

She hadn't given Elza Kanzaki her e-mail address yet, but if necessary, she could use the messaging system in *GGO*, so the result was the same.

Now, who is intruding on my leisure time? she wondered, looking at the sender of the text.

"Karen! Huge tidings!"

It was Saki.

"Uh-huh? What is it?" she replied mechanically, scrolling down the screen with her phone held straight above her upturned face.

"Did you see the news?"

"Huh? About what?" she mused aloud to the screen, continuing down through the body of the message.

"It's happening! Next month! The span is staying brief!"

"What is? What's happening?"

"You'll be entering, I assume? This time! It'll happen for sure! I'm looking forward to it! Gosh! I'm so pumped up!"

"About what? What am I entering?"

Her mind was so utterly relaxed that it wasn't functioning at all. Nothing passed through her head other than the mechanical instruction to her thumb to keep scrolling down.

"This time, I'll kill you for sure!"

When she saw the final line, Karen yelped, "Hyurk?"

Her fingers slipped, and the smartphone obeyed the laws of gravity to fall a few inches downward.

Gonk!

"Ouch!"

It bounced off Karen's forehead on a corner and plopped onto the bedsheet nearby.

Now Karen was rolling around atop her bed for a very different reason.

"Ooooh, it hurts, it hurts!"

At that very moment, somewhere else among the twenty-three wards of Tokyo, a pretty woman climbed into an expensive German SUV in an underground parking garage surrounded by concrete.

She was in her early twenties, skinny and petite, with straight black hair long enough to reach her bottom. Her outfit was extremely casual, just jeans and a T-shirt.

The woman hopped into the back and plopped onto the expensive leather seat.

Her name was Elza Kanzaki.

She was one of the most famous singer-songwriters in Japan at the moment, and much less known was that she was the person behind the crazed and deadly *GGO* character of Pitohui.

Elza promptly put on her seatbelt, leaned back against the seat, and closed her eyes.

"Shutting the door," a young man said just before it boomed

shut. He came around to the driver's seat on the right side, the motion rocking the vehicle.

The driver was a very handsome man in a clean-fitting navy-blue suit.

His name was Goushi Asougi.

He was an employee of Elza Kanzaki's talent agency, her personal driver, and probably her lover, as well as her servant or henchman or slave, or something along those lines.

In *GGO*, he was the massively buff and powerful man known as M.

The SUV quietly rolled into motion. It climbed the slope of the garage and out into the open street, where the sky dumped rain on the city.

Soon after they turned onto the big road, Goushi started talking to her from the front seat as he drove. "Nice work today. There's nothing left on your schedule. But separately, what you expected is coming to pass. There was just a news update about it."

In the back seat, Elza had her eyes shut, shapely lashes downcast; she almost looked asleep. Seconds after he spoke, her petite mouth opened to say only, "About what?"

"You must be tired…," her driver kindly said.

"Kind of. Well, whatever it is, I'm going to fall asleep once you explain it to me. When we get home, you have to carry me on your back up to my room, got it?" Elza told him.

Goushi hesistated. "Ah…well, once you hear what I have to say, you'll have a hard time sleeping, I think. Should it wait until you wake up?"

"Oh…? You're going to keep the current world-record holder for sleepiness, who was up all night, awake even longer? Say it. If it's true, I'll kick your ass later. And if you're lying, I'll kick your ass later," Elza said, eyes closed, voice pristine and beautiful. If any of her fans were to hear her, they'd be stunned and disappointed.

But she knew that, too, of course, and would never think of uttering her most private thoughts in public where anyone could hear.

The light ahead was red, and the SUV came to a stop. Without turning back to face her, Goushi obeyed her order.

"Then I'll tell you. The third Squad Jam, which everyone rumored would be coming soon, has been officially announced. It's going to be on Sunday the fifth of next month, starting around noo— Ghrlh!"

Elza's eyes snapped open. She bolted upright and smacked Goushi directly in the back of the neck with her skinny arm.

"Not while I'm driving, please! We're lucky it's a red light!" he protested. This made sense, because punching the back of a driver's neck was a very dangerous thing to do. Definitely one of those things that good little girls and boys should not do at home.

"Shut yer frickin' piehole! We're diving into *GGO* as soon as we get back!"

"I thought you were going to slee— Ghrlh!"

She punched him again. "How can I sleep now?! I'm entering! I'm doing SJ3! And so are you!"

"But…that's the day after the last night of the concert tour. Aren't you going to be exhausted?" Goushi said out of concern.

"As long as it's not the same day!" Elza promptly replied.

About two hours later, around five o'clock on Saturday evening.

"Yoo-hoo! Llenn! Long time no see!"

"Pito, it's been forev— Hrrgh!"

In a restaurant in the *GGO* city of Glocken, tall, muscular Pitohui clamped Llenn like a vise so hard that she felt like her insides were going to squirt out of her mouth.

Pitohui was dressed in her usual *GGO* outfit, a skintight navy-blue bodysuit. Angled, geometric tattoos adorned her cheeks. Her black hair was gathered into a tight ponytail in the back.

Llenn, too, wore her own trademark look of pink combat fatigues and pink hat. In fact, it was the only clothing she had in the game.

Pitohui squeezed her so hard it was practically strangulation, hurtling her friend's tiny body back and forth. "Wow, it really feels like it has been forever! Oh, you're just so cute! Did you shrink?"

"Gyaaa!"

"That's enough, Pito," said a man built like a mountain, wearing a T-shirt. If he hadn't done so, she probably *would* have strangled Llenn.

From there, Llenn, Pitohui, and M entered a private room where other players couldn't see or overhear them.

"Iced tea!" Pitohui ordered for Llenn. It popped out of the table at once. "Here we go! Cheers! Whoooo! So anyway, I can't wait to fight in SJ3!" she said, getting right to the point.

"Huh?" Llenn gaped, straw for her iced tea stuck to her lip. Pitohui held up a glass with a drink of some mysterious color and smiled. "I mean, that's what I wrote in that message. They're holding SJ3."

"Yeah, I know that! But I never wrote back with any indication I was signing up!"

"Oh? You don't want to? The honored champion and then runner-up hero who defeated *me* isn't going to tuck her tail between her legs and flee when I'm burning for revenge, is she? Is she?" Pitohui teased unpleasantly.

But Llenn wasn't that weak anymore. "I'm not taking that bait!" She wet her whistle with more iced tea and snapped back, "I'm tired of fighting against you! It's exhausting! I don't want to do it, if I have the choice! In fact, I definitely don't want to do it!"

"Aww, you're no fun."

"And more im-por-tant-ly! We don't have any reason to fight!"

"Aww."

"It's true! I'll hang out in the bar and root for you! I'll burn the image of your heroism into my retinas!"

Llenn sat back and took another sip from her straw, satisfied that she'd made an airtight case.

"Ahhh, I see your point. It's true; you don't really have a reason to fight me. I can understand that," Pitohui admitted.

"Oh?" Llenn's eyes went wide.

But she nearly spit out her tea when Pitohui said, "So let's play on the same team this time!"

"Huh?"

"You don't want to go against me, right? So we just have to be on the same team instead! We'll finally get to be in Squad Jam as teammates! That's so exciting! Hey, squaddie!"

"……But, but, but…," Llenn countered, yet Pitohui's grinning face got closer and closer. True to form, the smile was pleasantly malicious.

"Besides, you've broken one very important promise already, haven't you?"

"Pardon?" This time, Llenn really was confused. She'd fulfilled her promise to Pitohui in SJ2, so that really should have been the end of her commitments.

"Your battle against the Amazons!" Pitohui reminded her.

"Ah…"

It wasn't until that point that Llenn recalled the very reason she'd dropped her smartphone on her face two hours earlier. Pitohui was right; the battle she'd promised Saki, boss of the Amazons, had been delayed in SJ2 because of her own personal reasons.

Thanks to that, Pitohui was still alive here today. Llenn ignored the temptation to say *This is all your fault!* She had to find a way to fulfill her promise to Boss. But there was just one simple question to answer first.

"How did you know about that, Pito?"

She hadn't told anyone else about the promise she made in SJ2. There was a video archive, but there wouldn't be any voice audio. And Llenn couldn't imagine that the other girls had any connection to Pitohui.

"Huh? How did I know?" Pitohui repeated, baffled that Llenn wouldn't already be aware. "Because Miyu told me, obviously."

The face of the other person who had been present flickered through Llenn's mind like a storm. Miyu and Fukaziroh, two sides of the same coin, flipped back and forth, both smiling.

So unbeknownst to Karen, Miyu had gotten the contact info for Pitohui—make that Elza Kanzaki—and had been carrying on a correspondence secretly.

It was quite the opposite reaction to Karen's after meeting Elza in person, when Elza had French-kissed Karen and caused her to distance herself out of a sense of personal peril.

"Th-th-that...bitch!" Llenn howled, but there was nothing she could do about it now.

"So give it up, Llenn. If you're able to get to the bar that day to watch, it means you don't have anything else going on, right?"

"Urgh..."

"And you need to fulfill your promise to the Amazons, so you'll take part in SJ3. You need powerful teammates to fight a powerful team, so that means me and M...and why not invite Miyu? She can just convert over again!"

"Booo..." Llenn pouted. The plans were coming together over her protests.

"Six members is the max for a squad...but we're all tough, so I bet four will be enough!"

"Hrrm..."

"Oh, stop sulking! Let's fight on the same side! It's a game, okay? A game! Just a normal game! Let's just have fun with it and make the most of this opportunity!"

So said the very person who had ensured that the previous two times, Llenn *couldn't* just enjoy a normal game and have fun with it. Her smile was radiant.

"......"

Llenn didn't know whether to be furious or to laugh.

✳   ✳   ✳

Whether she wanted to or not, Llenn was going to participate in SJ3. In the coming days, other SJ-obsessed squads had some thoughts on the matter.

*   *   *

"Whoo-hoo! Karen's going to team up with Pitohui and Fuka-ziroh this time!"

The members of SHINC, the all-girls high school gymnastics team led by Saki, were beside themselves with excitement.

"Yes! Revenge match!"

"Payback for SJ1!"

"The big-time fight we've been waiting for!"

"We're just getting started!"

"Let's kill 'em!"

They were dressed in their school uniforms and shouting bloody murder on the sidewalk in broad daylight, which caused mild alarm among the other pedestrians.

"SJ3 time, baby! What are we doing, boys?"

In their usual group chat, the collection of machine-gun aficionados spread across Japan known as ZEMAL, the All-Japan Machine-Gun Lovers, were similarly pumped up.

"We're doin' it!"

"I'm in! And this time, I'm keepin' an eye above us, too!"

"If there's a reason *not* to play, I wanna hear it."

"I would pawn off my own parents to enter this tournament! How much do you think they'll give me?"

"Awesome! Then I'll get us registered! But…we can have one more person, so it sure would be nice to round out the group."

"I agree, but it's a bit late for that."

"We gotta find someone who loves machine guns as much as us? Tough assignment."

"Got it. That'll be our homework for next time. This round, we enter as five!"

"Okay! Give us your protection, god of machine guns!"

"Yes! Bless us, Open Bolt!"

"Please, we beg of you! Open Bolt!"

"OB, our god!"

"OB! OB! OB!"

And so a new cult religion was born.

"And that's why I called this impromptu meeting."

The all-male MMTM team, full title Memento Mori, had lost to M and Llenn the first time around, and Pitohui alone the last time. Today they were having an in-*GGO* meetup.

"We're not doing any hunting activities today, just having a discussion."

They were in a private room in a pub in Glocken. They wore the same thing they had on in SJ2, an old Swedish camo pattern of straight lines and angles in green shades. Apparently, it had become their trademark look.

"I'm thinking that we should enter as a team again. Is there anyone who absolutely can't make July 5th?" asked their handsome leader. The other five around the table all said they were available.

"Good! Then let's win this time!" he said, slamming a fist into his open palm. "Squad Jam's getting a name for itself, too, so we might have some talented new opponents—but for now, we're dealing with that gorilla's band of Amazons; they've got good teamwork. There's the little pink shrimp who ya can't hit for the life of ya, and then crazy Pitohui's team. Whenever we're able to get together, we will focus on tactics and practice designed to counter these specific teams."

One of the men, who wore shades indoors, said, "Pardon my interruption."

His name was Lux. He used the 5.56 mm G36K assault rifle. He was the one who drowned in the lake in SJ1 and got his head cut off by Pitohui's lightsword in SJ2.

"For a while now, I've actually been thinking of changing jobs to a sniper role."

"Oh?" said the leader.

The rest of the team looked at Lux, who explained, "In SJ, much of the combat happens in more open environments than you'd expect going into the event. I think it'd be good to have at least one sniper who can hit a target at twenty-five hundred feet. So I'm considering giving up the G36K for an MSG90. With an automatic sniper rifle, I can provide long-distance support for the rest of the team. But I wanted to get everyone's approval first, since that will change our tactical style."

As Lux said, the MSG90 was an automated sniper rifle that would shoot continuously just from pulling the trigger. Like the G36K, it was made by Heckler & Koch (HK) from Germany. The body was based on the G3 assault rifle, with an enlarged 7.62 mm caliber barrel. That was the same size as M's M14 EBR.

So it could be used for sniping, and its automatic fire could work in mid- or close-range situations as well. It was an almighty weapon very close in usage and specs to the M14 EBR overall.

"I see…"

The team leader thought this over. To this point, the team's machine gunner, named Jake, had taken on the limited role of sniper. His HK21 was based on the G3, too, and could be switched to semi-auto mode. It also had a scope for long-distance aiming.

But the principal purpose of a machine gun was to lay down a hail of fire. It could never match a sniper rifle for precision, so the scope had a low zoom and couldn't give an accurate reading at a distance.

Having just one sniper on the team would give them a much bigger advantage in open spaces than they had at the moment. Lux was also the team's biggest real-life gun fanatic, and his aim was good.

On the other hand, they would be going from five close-range storm troopers to four. A 20 percent loss of power was no laughing matter. They would definitely need to practice as a team under any new strategic lineup.

All decisions have their upsides and downsides. Nothing was pure good or bad.

In four seconds, the team leader arrived at his decision.

"Let's do it!"

"I can? You sure?" Lux said, double-checking.

The leader told him and the rest of the team, "Everything is a new challenge. If it doesn't work out, then it doesn't work out. You can blame me for making a bad decision."

The other five grinned. They knew that *their* decision to make him the leader was the right one. The quickness of decision and the responsibility to claim fault if it went wrong were the marks of a quality leader.

"What's the plan? Are we entering again...?"

At that moment, in a different pub elsewhere in *GGO*, more players discussed signing up for SJ3. This group was made up of seven men and one woman. The men sported a variety of hair-styles, but the solitary woman stood out even more thanks to hers—in a brilliant-green color.

They were the team known as KKHC, the Kita no Kuni Hunters Club; *Kita no Kuni* meaning "from the north."

This group of real-life hunting companions had formed their own squadron in *GGO* for the purpose of improving their hunting and shooting skills in a safe virtual environment. They wore matching jackets in a camouflage pattern that looked like realistic trees, better suited for hunting than combat.

Last time, four of the men and the one woman here had been available on the day of Squad Jam and entered on a lark.

"Boy, we sure got creamed...," complained a middle-aged man with a receding hairline. He was right—the results had been brutal.

It was their first experience with personal combat. They played conservatively, utilizing their sniping strengths to pick off a number of enemy teams, but suggesting an alliance with Pitohui's deadly squad after that was a clear lapse in judgment.

She turned them down, then shot them in the back as they left.

The four men all died on the spot without a chance to shoot back. Only the green-haired girl, Shirley, escaped alive. She put up an excellent fight on her own and even got a hit on the hateful Pitohui.

However, in the end, she was unable to finish the job and avenge her teammates. The pink shrimp who got runner-up shot her in the head. Game over.

After several moments of silence, a young man who was among the SJ2 participants said, "Well, I dunno… I mean…we don't *have* to play, do we?"

The room softened a bit. He had earned their warm gratitude for being the one to step up and suggest the thing they all wanted but were afraid to say. With the ice broken, he continued, "I mean, team combat is fun and all, but we're in *GGO* to practice our hunting accuracy, not to get better at killing people, you know? So we can just—"

Wham! Hands slapped the table.

"Weak!"

That was Shirley, who got to her feet. She snarled, exposing white canines.

"Aren't you angry? That woman's going to be in it again! It's the perfect chance to slaughter her right in front of everyone! Don't you at least want revenge against her? To blast a hole right through her head and score a satisfying clean kill? Don't you have the guts to pit yourself against a powerful enemy?"

Furious passion exuded from her every pore, down to the tips of her green hair. Her teammates could practically see an aura rising, despite it being a video game, incapable of simulating spiritual power.

In short, the men were freaked out.

"Erm…"

"Well…uhhh…"

"Gosh…"

"I dunno…"

Collectively, the men had the same thought: *That's weird; weren't you the one who held out until the last moment on trying SJ2, claiming that it wasn't proper for someone who used guns in real life to practice shooting players in the game...?*

And yet, none of them had the guts to say this out loud, so they just sat in silence.

"I'm going to enter!" Shirley yelled. "Who else? Is anyone with me?"

She stared down her companions.

Elsewhere at that moment, a player spoke to five teammates who were leading the way. "You'll be entering, right? Because I'm in. I can't wait for it."

They were in the wilderness of *GGO*. The game's setting was said to be a post-apocalyptic Earth, when a spaceship returned with human beings after the planet had been rendered uninhabitable by war.

Even the atmosphere was ruined here. The sky at midday was bloodred, and the earth was a blasted, arid wasteland. In the distance, skyscrapers stood bent in various stages of slow collapse.

The speaker was a handsome player with short black hair, wearing black combat gear with four cylindrical pouches on the chest and a plastic pistol holster on the right hip.

His—no, her—name was Clarence.

While she looked like a handsome man and spoke with the characteristic roughness of a man, the player was a woman. The system that AmuSphere VR games used prevented players from playing as characters whose sexes differed from their real-life identities.

Clarence had her first taste of Squad Jam action in the previous event. Her squad chose to join forces with others inside a giant dome packed with jungle trees and undergrowth. Their strategy was to beat the powerhouse teams like Llenn's LF, SHINC, and MMTM with the strength of numbers alone.

Three teams totaling eighteen members formed a net that succeeded in catching the pink shrimp's team—they just weren't good enough to win.

In the midst of an unexpected pink smokescreen, the tiny player darted back and forth, finishing off enemies one by one. It was the Massacre in the Dome and was the cause of much celebration for the players watching the event live.

By coincidence, Clarence had the chance to briefly talk with Llenn, and in the end, she gave the other girl her leftover ammo magazines, just moments before she was shot and killed by MMTM.

Rocking against her back as she walked across the desert was an AR-57.

It was quite an eccentric gun. It had the lower receiver—meaning the bottom and back half—of an M16 but the upper receiver of a different gun entirely, making it a sort of firearm chimera.

As for the upper receiver, it was actually nearly identical to Llenn's P90. It had the magazine on top in the same way and fired special 5.57 mm rounds.

In *GGO* and in the real world, these two guns were the only kinds that used this type of magazine. It was the only reason she was able to provide Llenn with all that ammo.

"I'd like to see that squirt again! And this time, I'll use every dirty trick in the book and win fair and square! I wanna shoot her in the back! I wanna shoot her cute little butt! I wanna stick the muzzle into her mouth and pull the trigger!" Clarence trilled happily. In the meantime, her teammates, who were outfitted with a variety of camo and weapons, made faces of disgust.

Even the most clueless of people could tell that they clearly did not want to take part in SJ3. Or perhaps it was that they didn't want to take part in SJ3 *with Clarence*.

"So we're all in this one together, right? Shall I sign us up? Same lineup as last time, okay?" Clarence said, all in a rush.

"Nope! I'm busy that day."

"So am I. Gotta pass on this one."

"Me too."

"Ditto."

The four all declined, none of them turning back to look at Clarence.

It was often the case that players in *GGO* spoke without looking one another in the face. Not because of any antisocial desire to avoid others, but because you had to be on the lookout for monsters and enemy players.

In this case, however, it was perfectly accurate to say that none wanted to look at Clarence. Or show their expressions, either.

Clarence trotted over to the closest victim. "What about you, Sam?" she said as she grabbed his shoulders. His avatar was that of a dark-skinned Middle Eastern man. He turned to her. His name was Sam. Just Sam.

While his features were well-composed, the body was his avatar, and it exhibited his mental state quite faithfully, twisting with hesitation and unease.

"Um...I..."

"Be a man and man up! Are you busy that day?"

"No, but I...," he said, withering under the pressure.

"Then it's settled." Clarence released her grip and patted his shoulder. There was resignation on his face.

She turned to the rest of the group and said happily, "Hey, everyone! I'll be entering with Sam! At least show up for the preliminary round, okay!"

There had been a preliminary selection round in SJ2, and there would probably be one this time, too. It would be tough to get through the prelims with just the two of them, so her request was a "friendly" invitation for the rest to join for that round.

The other four did not respond. Without breaking her smile, Clarence said, "If you don't, I'm going to spill the beans about you-know-what."

"Oh, I'm in!" "Of course I'm there!" "Why wouldn't I be?" "I was hoping to participate in the prelims!" they all stammered at once, talking over one another and making it hard to distinguish their words.

What was crystal clear, however, was that Clarence had some kind of dirt on her male teammates.

*   *   *

The teams hoping to take part in SJ3 filed their entry forms one after the other, as soon as they were able. The passion for Squad Jam hadn't diminished over the downtime. The prizes for landing among the top ranks, while not as deluxe as the last one, included guns, medicine, and a variety of ammunition.

Even without the promise of a deluxe prize, the offer of a special exclusive map that you couldn't find elsewhere in GGO was the kind of thing that struck the gamer's soul. The interior jungle of the last event was a good example of that.

Another perk was the chance to engage in team combat with some like-minded friends. And even better, they recorded live footage for the pub audience, so you also had the fun of seeing the video of your team kicking ass (or getting its ass kicked) afterward.

Among the player base, there was one rule in particular that struck up conversation. What did it mean?

SJ3 essentially carried over all the rules of SJ2. It would be a thirty-team battle-royale event, with Satellite Scans every ten minutes that displayed the location of each team's leader. The four top finishers from last time would each be given a bye. The competition would take place on a map ten kilometers to a side, or a bit over six miles. All dead bodies would remain in place as indestructible objects for ten minutes.

But this time, there was one mysterious rule added to the list.

"By the sponsor's suggestion, at the point that only six to eight teams remain, a new rule will be announced and put into place. It is designed to be enjoyable for both participants and viewers. Please look forward to it."

There were absolutely no details as to what it might be. No hints were given or questions answered. There was even a warning on the form saying that if you didn't like it, you didn't have to enter.

Why would it take place when six to eight teams were left? What was the reason for the range between those numbers? There was no way to know ahead of time.

Normally, you might react with anger. *Who's gonna take part in a game where you don't know the rules before you start? Harrumph!* But in this case, nobody withdrew their application on account of the new rule.

For one thing, in a chaotic battle like SJ, it would be very difficult to survive until only eight teams remained, so this wasn't a serious issue to the majority of the players entering. More important was just lasting that long.

And to the teams with the skill and potency to last to the final eight, it was a trivial issue.

"What's the use in worrying about it? It's not like they're going to install a rule banning machine guns! OB!" said someone in the Machine-Gun Lovers.

"Who cares? Whatever it is, we'll adapt appropriately when the time comes," said the leader of MMTM.

"No matter what happens, we're teammates, and we won't back down," said Boss from SHINC.

"I'm not worried in the least. If anything, something different might spice up the proceedings," said Pitohui.

Karen told Miyu about it during a call to Hokkaido and got a very muted reaction.

"Hmm, I wonder what it is. In one of the games I played, they would do stuff like bump weapon durability all the way back up to max for the final battle to make it more exciting."

"Ooooh. You think they'd refill all your ammo or something?"

"I'm more excited about the chance to hold Rightony and Leftania again soon!"

That was about the extent to which they dealt with whatever the new rule might be.

CHAPTER 2

SECT.2

The Third Squad Jam

CHAPTER 2
The Third Squad Jam

July 5th, 2026.

The start of the third Squad Jam was rapidly approaching.

Like before, the main gathering place to follow the tournament was a big pub in the city of Glocken. It was on the ground floor of a big building, but the interior was large enough to hold several hundred people easily. There were plenty of tables, counters, and even private rooms. Huge screens were hung on the walls and from the ceiling.

Altogether, thanks in part to *GGO*'s American origins, the place looked like a wild saloon from a Hollywood movie and not at all like a cramped, intimate Japanese bar.

The participants in the battle gathered here, as did the audience who drank and enjoyed the live feed. Ten minutes after they died, defeated players would return here, too.

As expected, the number of participating teams in SJ3 rose to a total of fifty-seven, a modest expansion of the forty-nine from last time.

Three of those teams were given seeded ranking, putting them past the preliminary round.

First, there was the winning team of SJ2, T-S.

Everyone remembered them. They were the team decked out

in protectors that made them look like sci-fi soldiers. They had bided their time in SJ2 and seized victory at the end in the most improbable way.

For nearly the entire game, they rode atop the castle walls on bicycles. They shot the Machine-Gun Lovers from atop the wall. When Llenn and Fukaziroh were nearly dead from winning their battle against Pitohui, T-S shot them full of bullets from a long distance. The team as a whole suffered *zero* damage.

It was a strategic victory, to be sure, but it was not a popular outcome at all with the fans, who had come expecting a white-knuckle victory.

They recognized this and did not reappear in the bar following the end of SJ2—but here they were, proudly proclaiming their intention to fight again in SJ3.

The second-seeded team was called LPFM, containing Llenn, the champion and runner-up of the previous two Squad Jams, and Pitohui, who had won third place the last time out.

This was the name of Llenn's team for SJ3. It was simply the initials of its four members: Llenn, Pitohui, Fukaziroh, and M. It was so named by Pitohui, and that was the official team name, not an abbreviated tag.

"Ell-Pee-Eff-Em? It's too hard to say, Pito!"

"I'm glad you noticed, Llenn! That's part of the plan! Every time an enemy team reads our name off the scanner, they'll have to say the entire 'Ell-Pee-Eff-Em' name! Who knows, maybe they'll bite their tongues and suffer damage! Not all combat happens down the barrel of a gun!"

"Oh, really…"

Since Llenn's team and Pitohui's team, the previous second- and third-place finishers, were on the same team this time, there were only three seeded teams.

The final seed belonged to SHINC, the fourth-place squad. They were the familiar team of Amazons. Only Karen and Miyu knew that, in real life, they were adorable little teenage gymnasts.

The other fifty-four squads had gone through the preliminary round the night before, Saturday evening. By coincidence, it produced exactly the number of teams needed for the final, so there would be no loser's bracket—only the winning teams advanced. Like SJ2, the prelim battles were one-on-one team fights on a long, narrow map.

In those circumstances, experience and talent typically won out, so nearly all the teams that had already played in Squad Jam survived and moved on.

The quickest team to win and advance, by far, ended up being MMTM.

After eleven o'clock, the crowd in the bar began to swell noticeably. The deadline to arrive was 11:50, and that was a very hard cutoff—not a second later would be tolerated. The earlier you were there, the more time you had to eat and drink and strategize ahead of time, so the place was already buzzing.

With each new team entering the building, the audience that had gathered to enjoy the proceedings (or who had no choice but to enjoy them) murmured a little louder. It was like the entrances for a wrestling or boxing match, only without the snappy music.

When a particularly powerful squad entered, the muttering in the bar calmed down, replaced by cheers or whispers under the breath. All of this was the same as in the previous Squad Jam.

"Hey, look at them…"

Some observant member of the crowd pointed out a group of five especially burly men. Their team had no unified camo wear, and their guns and equipment were stored in their virtual inventory to keep them secret for now, but everybody knew who they were.

"Oh! Those are the machine gunners…"

Indeed, it was the lineup of ZEMAL. They'd failed out of SJ1 without anything to show for it, but they made good use of their situation in SJ2 and put up—rude as it might be to say—a better fight than anyone expected of them.

They were finished off when they failed to detect T-S attacking from atop the wall, but sixth out of thirty was a very respectable finish.

Every member of their squad used a machine gun, giving them significant firepower and a major ammo stock, which could prove very formidable if they were blessed with a good starting location.

What kind of entertainment were they likely to bring the audience this time?

More and more teams from SJ2 entered the bar.

First, there was the team that got wiped by MMTM on the side of the snowy mountain, where the last surviving member had his own camera so he could provide live commentary.

He had uploaded the commentary video to the Internet under the title "Battling Hard in SJ2! Alas, I Couldn't Really Hear the Pained Screams of My Dying Friends on the Snowy Plain."

His admirable death (that characterization was debatable) had earned him numerous condolences in the comments field. He had declared his intention to do another round of commentary this time, and many fans were eagerly awaiting the results.

Next was the team that used the optical guns, victims of Fuka-ziroh's grenade bombardment in SJ2. Because virtually every player wore items called anti-optical defense fields that minimized the power of optical guns, they were considered nearly useless in PvP combat. These folks were the only ones who had ever used them in Squad Jam.

Would they stick to their guns (literally) this time?

The question would be: How could they take advantage of the long range, high accuracy, and room for extra weapons and energy packs, given their light weight?

In addition, there was the military history–buff team called the New Soldiers (NSS) who based their loadout and uniforms on Imperial Japanese officers, American Vietnam-War soldiers, and other distinct looks throughout history.

Their dedication to cosplay was so high and intense that their table stood out like a sore thumb among the others around them.

Finally, one of the big players arrived.

"Oh! Someone guide the contenders to their table!" joked someone near the door. The pub quieted down when they saw who had arrived: the six-man MMTM squad, one of the top over-all teams in the event, wearing their trademark Swedish camo. The men had menacing looks in their eyes (except for the one wearing sunglasses).

Although the people in the pub would not be aware of this, Team MMTM had over the last month undergone even fiercer training than before. The team leader had chosen to forego the fourth Bullet of Bullets, the huge individual battle-royale tourna-ment, in favor of focusing on SJ3 instead.

Lux had acquired his MSG90, as promised. He had also earned as much of a sniper's skill as possible, to allow him to prevent his pulse from racing, give him the ability to craft high-precision ammo, and so on.

And of course, with plenty of shooting practice, his long-distance aim got dramatically better. Anything within 2,500 feet in windless, good conditions was in his kill zone.

With one less assault rifle member, the remaining four, including the leader, rebalanced their team play. Each one of them needed to carry more ammo, too.

Now they were ready. But since their only chance to use their new team composition against a live enemy had been the prelims, and they made record-setting short work of their opponent, they would essentially be live-testing it out in SJ3.

But they were ready for that. They wanted to win—and they wanted revenge against Pitohui after the way she'd annihilated them last time.

The audience certainly hadn't forgotten that close-quarters bat-tle inside the huge log house at the end of SJ2. MMTM's assault on the building left the four masked men on Pitohui's team dead, despite a valiant effort.

At that point, it was an interior battle of six on two, MMTM's forte. It was a battle they absolutely should have been able to win, but Pitohui alone was successful at completely overturning their advantage.

They had also lost to Llenn and M in SJ1, so there was a score to settle there, too. And with all three of them on the same team, that was just fine and dandy with MMTM.

The potential rematch between MMTM and Pitohui's squad was the biggest draw for the audience of SJ3.

Once MMTM had taken their seats, two more teams with female players entered the building in succession.

The first one featured a handsome player in black fatigues whom anyone who had watched Llenn's battles in SJ2 would remember. She was the one in the massacre inside the dome who ended up getting shot by MMTM.

That was about the extent of their recognition, though. There was absolutely no hush that came over the crowd. It was hard to say how many of the people in the room even realized that she was female.

Clarence didn't seem bothered, though. She turned to Sam and said, "Well, I guess that about sums up our talent level, huh? Nobody pays attention to us when we walk into the room."

"Huh…," murmured Sam, who wore mottled brown-and-green camo. They took seats near the door of the pub. It was just the two of them this time. The entire team showed up for the preliminary round, and they beat their new-to-SJ opponent to advance, but only the pair of them were entering the final.

It was essentially an unwinnable fight. While Llenn and M had won the first Squad Jam as a duo, they were also an exception to common sense.

Sam could hardly be blamed for his lack of enthusiasm. Clarence told him, "We're gonna kick ass, all right? We do as we planned once it starts. Remember?"

"Ahhh…," Sam murmured once again. It wasn't clear whether that was an affirmative answer or just a sigh.

Right on the heels of Clarence came another team.

"Oh, those are the ones who got whacked last time," someone muttered.

It was the five-person team named KKHC, whom Pitohui had shot in the back in SJ2. The group included four men and one woman, green-haired Shirley. They all wore their characteristic hunting jackets. It was the only gear they owned.

"That chick… She was the one who nailed Pitohui, right? She's got guts," someone whispered. It was true; only Shirley and Llenn had inflicted any damage on Pitohui the last time around.

The audience couldn't see the hit points of the SJ participants. So when Pitohui took a shot to the head and survived, they just assumed that the bullet had only grazed her skull.

In fact, Pitohui had been a hair away from instant death. Her remaining points had been so low they had been visible simply as a sliver on the bar. Pitohui had survived only by the skin of her teeth; no one but she and her teammates knew how close it had been.

KKHC walked through the bustling bar and into the nearest private room. They sat around a table and ordered some drinks.

"Hey, Shirley, now that we're here, we're all in…but do we even stand a chance?" one of the men asked, his expression skeptical.

Another man said, "We haven't even practiced our teamwork or coordinated plays. And Squad Jam's a team battle. Can we actually beat a team who knows how to work together?"

Their skepticism was ironic, considering that after they had beaten their first enemies in SJ2, those very same men had said things like "Hey, given our skill, you think we might actually get pretty far in this?" and "Yeah, I bet. It's gonna be a bloodbath."

KKHC had chosen to enter SJ3 as a result of Shirley's demanding enthusiasm, but they barely made it through their prelim battle.

Their opponent was a six-person team with assault rifles and machine guns. But because they'd started playing to practice their real-life hunting, all of KKHC used bolt-action rifles, which had to be manually reloaded after each shot. It was the only weapon they used.

They'd eked out a victory thanks to Shirley's sniping. Since they could snipe without using a bullet line in the first place, their aim was excellent, if nothing else. The key to victory beyond that was simply keeping their wits about them.

In that regard, Shirley succeeded. While her teammates panicked at the hail of bullets coming from the enemy, she maintained her ground as the opponents charged, shooting and shooting with demonic coldness.

Her teammates couldn't help asking her, "Since when did you get so good at PvP combat? And…what are those bullets…?"

Shirley answered matter-of-factly, "I played on my own whenever I had time. I tried fighting some monsters, but I also fought players. I'd set an ambush for a squadron, then snipe until my magazine went empty. After that, I ran. I made the bullets."

"……"

No wonder they were flabbergasted. For all her vehemence about not wanting to shoot people, it turned out that she was actively going out and hunting down other players to kill them.

The fiercest member of this team was not any of the men, who had gone soft and submissive since SJ2, but Shirley.

In their private room, Shirley glared at her teammates and assured them, "Don't worry. I've got a strategy in mind that I think will be effective. It suits us, and it'll let us act to our hearts' desire."

It sounded reassuring enough, and the expressions on the men's faces softened a bit. If Shirley was the toughest member of the team right now, and she said so, then they could probably lean on her for guidance.

"So I want you to follow my commands," she said.

The rest of them nodded.

At about 11:35, the monitors in the bar were playing an interview with the tournament's sponsor, a novelist in his fifties. It was a recording, not a live interview.

Yes, it was the same clinically gun-obsessed man who sponsored the first Squad Jam. He was an unsightly fellow who worked under the impression that his unkempt facial hair made him look cool.

He fell into the rare case of a player whose real-life identity was known, but whose avatar in *GGO* was still a mystery. In the interview, he was carrying on about how someone else had sponsored SJ2 out from under his nose, but that he was so excited to be putting on the event this time. He certainly wasn't acting his age.

At least he was aware that his SJ1 grand prize of a "signed set of novels" had been poorly received, so he gave up and admitted that the prize this time would be in-game *GGO* items.

When the interviewer asked him about the special rule, he made a theatrical show of saying "Well, actually…whoops! Can't say that yet" and shook his head.

"Yeah, yeah, nice acting," said someone in the crowd.

"He came up with the rule, right? He seems like a messed-up guy, so I bet it'll be a messed-up rule."

"Is there a single gun freak in the world who has a healthy personality? The answer is no."

"Coming from you? I'm convinced. You would know."

"Exactly. What can I say? It's a skill."

The audience didn't seem very impressed with their benefactor.

*   *   *

Around 11:40 AM.

Nearly all the participating squads were present, and there was a larger audience gathered than in past instances. The bar was rocking, and there was a festive air in the room.

Once again, there was a pool going to guess how many shots (and optical energy bursts) would be fired overall during the battle. No one had guessed it exactly right the last two times.

Of course, guessing an exact integer five digits or higher might as well be picking a lottery number. Still, it was the best thing they could do without an actual betting book on the winner.

As for the previous champions, T-S, they had not arrived yet.

"I'm amazed they had the guts to enter again!"

"I can't wait to boo them to their faces!"

"Don't be annoying. Although I *will* pray they lose this time!"

"I can't believe what they did to my poor Llenn and Fukaziroh!"

"I know I pointed this out last time, but they're not *yours*," argued someone from the audience in the bar. But unbeknownst to them, the members of T-S were actually present and sitting at a table.

"Guess it was the right call to dress light."

"For sure."

"Nobody's figured it out."

In fact, they were having an entire pre-game meal, with food and drinks spread out in a sumptuous array—as people within earshot loudly disparaged them.

The reason they went unnoticed was simple: all the members wore generic combat gear and none of the characteristic bulky armor they had on before. They were enjoying themselves, knowing that nobody was aware of their identities.

A man wandered over to their table, dressed in woodland-pattern camo and a red beret. He said quietly, "Hey, you guys…"

Eek! We're busted! they thought, tensing up.

But the man only said, "You're participants, not spectators, right?"
Taken aback, one of the T-S members said, "Huh? Well, yeah…"
"I knew it. Here, read this." The man left them a message card, an item about the size of a stamp. Any player who touched it would receive a written message; it was essentially a letter. You could also place the item into an envelope and hand it over that way.

The man left without waiting for a reaction of any kind. Confused, the T-S members took turns tapping the card. Then they opened game windows invisible to other people, so no one could see them reading.

"……"

Six breaths were held in unison.

After a few seconds of reading, the message card automatically vanished, to avoid leaving evidence behind. At the same time, a separate item appeared in the inventory of the team members.

11:46 AM.

The participants of SJ3 had to be inside the bar by ten minutes to the hour. That was the point at which they would automatically be teleported to the waiting area.

One of the toughest squads in the competition showed up with four minutes to go. It was SHINC, dressed in camo with a spray of fine green dots. Runners-up of SJ1. Fourth place in SJ2. A team with the results to back up their reputation as fearsome Amazons.

"Here they are!"

"Whoo! It's about time!"

"Get 'em, ladies! You're gonna win this one!" the crowd roared as the women strode into the building.

Walking in the lead was a smaller woman with narrow eyes and short silver hair. Her name was Tanya, and she was the point woman on the team, the speedy attacker who took front position in battle.

She used a Bizon submachine gun. Her job was to wave this gun around, with its fifty-three-round cylindrical magazine of 9 mm bullets, to disturb and harass the enemy. For a sidearm, she carried a 9 mm Strizh automatic pistol.

After Tanya, who ran point in battle and into the building, was a woman with wavy blond hair and sunglasses, laughing with her teammate. That glamorous foreign actress type was Anna.

She was one of the team's two snipers, who used a semiautomatic Dragunov sniper rifle. She was also the prettiest avatar of the bunch. Many of the men in the room stopped what they were doing to stare.

Anna's conversation partner was Sophie, the sturdy dwarf of a woman. She looked like she could beat everyone with body slams alone. She used the devastating PKM machine gun as her weapon—in SJ1, that is. In SJ2, she gave up her favorite weapon to be a mule for SHINC's best weapon—and one of the greatest in *GGO*, period.

Within her inventory, she'd been hauling the PTRD-41 Anti-Tank Rifle. It was a beast of a gun with a seven-foot length that shot massive 14.5 mm bullets.

SHINC used this weapon to fire directly on M's special shield, rendering it structurally useless. The audience could still vividly remember the string of roaring blasts in that bombardment battle—as well as the role Sophie played in it.

Strolling behind them was a tall, thin woman with black hair and a green beanie. She was Tohma, the team's other sniper. Normally, she used a Dragunov with a special adjustible scope, but when Sophie brought out the PTRD-41, it was Tohma who fired it.

SHINC's secret weapon struck fear into the hearts of their opponents—and they were sure to use it without mercy, whenever possible. It was so powerful, after all. A devastating bullet could fly in from nearly invisible distances at any moment. And the closer it was, the harder it could punch through armored surfaces. Steel plates might be a stout defense under ordinary circumstances, but not against that monster.

"It's scary, man…," muttered one of the SJ3 contestants, quietly enough that they couldn't hear.

The man seated next to him said, "It's not fair, having an anti-tank rifle. Don't shoot that at people."

"Yeah, exactly."

"There's no kindness to it at all."

"Yeah, exactly."

Next came the fifth member of SHINC, whose short red hair and freckled face made her look older than she was, like a middle-aged woman from the cramped urban backstreets. Her name was Rosa.

She, too, used a PKM and carried a large supply of ammo and backup barrels in a huge backpack to great effect in both SJ1 and SJ2. As the team's only machine gunner this time around, she was sure to offer lots of backup firepower.

Lastly came the supremely powerful leader of the Amazons, a huge woman standing over six feet tall. Her face was menacing and, combined with her size, made her look positively gorilla-like. On the other hand, the pigtails were a feminine touch.

This was Eva, commonly known as Boss, the captain of the squad.

She used a silenced sniper rifle, the Vintorez. It was not just a regular gun with a sound suppressor or silencer stuck on after the fact, but a weapon built to be silent from the body to the ammo cartridges. It was a remarkably quiet gun, capable of killing targets very close by without them even hearing it. Like Tanya, she also carried a Strizh pistol in a hip holster.

SHINC had a certain combat pattern they liked to use that practically guaranteed victory. With perfect teamwork, they would first gain a positional advantage over their enemy, then lead with a crisp, violent hail of machine-gun bullets, while the Dragunovs took aim and fired from safety.

Even if the target survived the attack, they would be unable to move. From there, Boss and Tanya would sneak around the other side and quickly pick off the opposing team one at a time with their silent weapons.

They could also execute the reverse to great effect. In that case, the machine gunners and snipers fired into empty space on purpose. The enemy, thinking their location was safe, would emerge in an attempt to get behind them, only to run smack into Boss and Tanya.

Their teamwork and coordination were so tremendously smooth that the people watching the event feed wondered how it was possible for anyone to be that well coordinated. Only Llenn and Fukaziroh knew the answer.

SHINC was clearly one of the favorites alongside MMTM in this event. The audience couldn't wait to see what they would do this time around.

It was late enough that all the tables were full, however, so they ended up walking past where MMTM were sitting.

"Hello there, ladies," the team leader greeted. He and Boss had set sparks flying shortly before SJ2, so everyone watched nervously, wondering what kind of verbal sparring might ensue.

"Oh, hi there," said Boss, stopping briefly, without any apparent malice.

He continued, "It was a shame we couldn't square off properly last time. It just never seems to be in the cards."

"Indeed. Well, that's lucky for you."

These teams had never traded direct gunfire in the tournament before. SHINC had laid down covering machine-gun fire to allow Llenn to escape last time, but MMTM had promptly withdrawn to safety.

"Let us endeavor to attract luck's favor this time, then. By the way," MMTM's leader said, changing the subject with a humorless smile. The eyes in his handsome face held no mirth in them. "Let me be honest. Our greatest enemy in this fight is not you. If we end up as the last two teams, then yes, but not until that point. The same is true of you, isn't it?"

"Ah, I see. It seems we think the same way," Boss answered, her face hard.

Neither team's biggest enemy was the other. They both had a higher priority target. In other words, there was an unspoken agreement being traded between them now: *If we're "unlucky" enough to cross paths before then, can we agree to withdraw in peace?*

Just then, a murmur ran through the crowd of the bar. It stemmed from near the entrance. Neither of them needed to look to know who it was.

"They're here…" "They're here…"

The words and timing were perfectly in sync out of their mouths.

The greatest foe of both teams had just arrived.

Just after the clock showed 11:48…

Llenn entered the doorway of the pub.

"Why does it always have to be just in the nick of time?!"

She wore her usual pink combat gear and hat, with a brown robe covering them up. "It's just getting ridiculous at this point! It's bad for my heart! You've got to be kidding me!"

Llenn was furious. She was in a prickly mood, with the person she was venting at just behind her. You couldn't blame her, though; in another hundred seconds, she would've been too late to enter the battle.

"Geeeez, I'm sorryyy. Listen, I'll buy you an iced tea. And any snacks you like!" protested Fukaziroh, who followed her inside. Like Llenn, she was small and dressed in a concealing robe. With the way the hood covered part of her face, she looked like some wise monkish sage. A very small one.

"As if we have time for that!" Llenn was still angry.

"Oh, what's the harm if we're a little bit late?" said Pitohui in her bodysuit.

Last came M, wearing a T-shirt. "Looks like we made it in time." The two of them seemed unconcerned that they'd just barely gotten through the door in time. They were as aloof and cool as always.

"Ugh…" Llenn sighed, robed shoulders slumping, quickly feeling absurd for being the only one angry.

Before SJ2 started, Miyu was late because of a stomachache due to eating ice cream just before diving. And once again, the group's tardiness in arriving was absolutely her fault.

Believe it or not, Miyu (or her avatar, Fukaziroh) was in *ALO* until earlier in the day. Until just moments ago, in fact.

She'd been on a major adventure with her *ALO* friends and had been playing practically nonstop, except for meal and bathroom breaks offline, since Saturday morning—without sleep.

It was a very unhealthy way to play. More than a few hours a day of full-diving was bad for the mind. And if you spent too much time in virtual reality overall, you might enter a very dangerous mental state where it became impossible to tell which side was real life.

"They like to say you should only play two hours of VR per day, but…when you're Miyu Shinohara, it's not a problem at all."

Her protests aside, the plan called for Fukaziroh to have a big, thrilling adventure with her *ALO* friends that wrapped up during the morning, giving her a few hours' time to take care of converting to *GGO*. It was a risky move, but they registered her name under their team because she had a record of *GGO* play in the past.

The adventure dragged on and on, however, leaving her with almost no time to spare. Since they couldn't meet up the day before, Llenn told her to be in Glocken at ten o'clock, a healthy buffer, and had all of Fukaziroh's gear in a cart waiting for her—but when she received no glimpse or word of her friend, she began to fret.

Pitohui and M, true to their word, contacted her right at eleven o'clock when they dived into *GGO*. They were greeted by a flustered, teary Llenn. "Oh no! Fukaziroh hasn't shown up! What should we do?!"

They waited together for over half an hour. At last, Fukaziroh showed up, freshly converted, and they raced into the pub as a group with less than two minutes to spare.

For a little while, she thought they'd have to play as a trio. She had given up Fukaziroh for dead. It worked out, and Llenn knew she should focus on the positives, but she was already exhausted.

"I'm tired... I'm dead tired..."

It was a bad way to start the big competition.

When Llenn walked through the door, the quieted bar erupted into cheers again.

"There she is!"

"Whoooooo!"

"It's about time!"

Even under the robe, her identity was obvious. The two tiny girls stood out, after all, and Pitohui and M behind them made no attempt whatsoever to disguise themselves.

"This has got to be the favorite to win..."

"It's practically cheating to have them together...," the audience said, quite honestly.

And who could blame them? It was a combination of the winners of SJ1 and the runners-up and third place of SJ2. The four members striding into the pub were each noteworthy in their way.

Llenn, the speedy, tiny target, who charged her enemies in a direct, disorienting fashion.

Fukaziroh, the pip-squeak with two very big and powerful multi-shot grenade launchers.

Pitohui, the cruel and all-around high-level woman who fought like she had a few screws loose.

M, the calm and brilliant sniper who didn't need a bullet line, with a shield that could deflect just about any bullet.

All of them were very high-powered. In fact, they each seemed to have dedicated their skill points to various unbalanced extremes. There were only four members, but each one was about as powerful as two other players. They might as well have been an eight-person team.

The audience could barely take the anticipation of what sort of success this squad might have and, more importantly, what kind of brutally wild and flashy mass slaughter they might produce.

As for the other SJ3 participants, they could barely take the anticipation of how famous they would be for beating a team straight from Hell like this one. Even if it probably wasn't going to happen.

"Whoo! Good luck, lady!"

"Can't wait!" cheered some admirers of Pitohui's.

"Thank you, thank you, you're too kind, how're you doing?" she replied, smiling and waving like a local politician in her election campaign vehicle. In fact, she had acted this way in SJ2, too, but nobody really knew who she was back then, so all she got were blank, annoyed stares. Now it was a much different story.

"Ooooh! There she is!"

"I love you! Kill 'em all!"

"I'm looking forward to this one!" they cheered, as though a pop idol had just walked into the building.

"Thank you, everyone!" Pitohui said, addressing the crowd as though she was a famous singer. Which, in fact, she was.

"Hey! She smiled at me!"

"No way, it was me!" giggled the spectators in the room.

"......"

The participants just glared. It was very easy to tell the difference.

I wonder where—?

Llenn was looking for someone. She spun around. She jumped.

At last, she found her woman. Even at a distance, it was hard to mistake that combination of huge stature and braided hair.

"Thank you for your patience, contestants. Teleportation to

the waiting area will begin in thirty seconds. Is everyone ready for battle?" said an announcement over the speaker.

The crowd began to cheer. "Good luck out there, Llenn!"

"Kick some ass!"

"You're lookin' tiny and cute today!"

But she didn't have enough time to favor them with her attention. Llenn trotted over to Boss in the last few seconds remaining.

Her watch said 11:49:50. There was no time left, but she had to get across this one message.

Llenn looked up at Boss. A smile was visible beneath her hood. "I'm here."

Boss greeted her with arms folded. Her stern face wore the kind of smile that would make a child burst into tears.

"I was hoping you'd show up."

The clock hit 11:50.

The teleportation process immediately turned the two into flashes of light that dissipated into thin air.

The waiting area was a dim, close-quarter area with not much more than floor that continued for an indeterminate distance. High in the air, hanging on nothing in particular, was a countdown that said REMAINING TIME: 09:55.

For ten minutes until the start of SJ3, the participants prepped their combat gear here and went over some brief tactical plans with their teammates. If they lost all their hit points in battle, meaning their character died, each player would be returned to this waiting area for another ten minutes before going back to the bar.

That was the same amount of time that the player's body would remain in the SJ3 map as an indestructible object. To pass the time, they could watch the live feed of the battle in the waiting room—or just log out of the game altogether, of course.

"Let's see…"

Llenn began preparing for battle, determined to make use of

the waiting time. By the third time in this event, she was used to the drill.

She waved an invisible conductor's wand with her left hand, bringing up a command window. With some button presses and icon slides, she first stashed away the robe, which she didn't need for Squad Jam. It silently vanished, making the pink shrimp pink again.

Next, she materialized her rationed items. Everyone in Squad Jam received three crucial emergency med kits and a Satellite Scan terminal.

The med kits were the only HP-recovering item in the event. They were large, syringe-like cylinders that could be stuck against any part of the body. One kit healed 30 percent of the user's health, but slowly, over the course of three minutes. A serious challenge of Squad Jam was that you couldn't heal quickly in the midst of battle.

The Satellite Scan terminal was a special device just for Squad Jam that showed a map of the terrain and, once every ten minutes, the location of other squads. Visually, it was pretty much just a smartphone.

It was so important that no one stood a chance without it, so the game designers made sure that the item was indestructible. Putting it in her shirt pocket in SJ1 actually saved Llenn's life. It helped that she was small and not particularly well-endowed.

Almost certainly because of that incident, the terminals were reprogrammed to allow bullets to pass through, starting in SJ2. It wasn't fair to go around intentionally taking advantage of that, after all.

Llenn placed her med kits into a thin pouch on the front of her body and stuck her terminal into her shirt pocket. She'd had to show Fukaziroh how to use it last time, but that wasn't necessary now.

Next she selected the EQUIP ALL GEAR command from her window. Utility belts appeared around her pink-camo outfit silently. They were nice and snug around her waist and shoulders, and the pouches for the long P90 ammo magazines materialized three on each hip.

She had her backup magazines in her virtual item storage. After nearly running out of ammo last time, she'd learned her lesson and stocked up with more: another fifteen, in fact. Her weight was just barely under the limit of what she could carry without a movement penalty based on her stats.

So she had one magazine in her gun, six at her sides, and fifteen in her inventory, for twenty-two in all. There were fifty rounds a pop, so that made 1,100 in total.

She also brought along the sound suppressor that she used to great effect last time. She didn't have it on yet because the shorter the gun barrel, the more maneuverable it was.

Naturally, she equipped the comm device that allowed her to talk to her teammates like a phone. She also brought a monocular with a distance measure on it.

But the gear wasn't done showing up. Next appeared Llenn's valuable sidearm, a vicious combat knife with a black blade that she kept behind her at her waist, where she could pull it out backhanded with her right hand. The knife had played a major part in her final battles of both SJ1 and SJ2. She would have lost both fights without it.

Lastly, the most crucial item of all, without which she couldn't fight at all: her main weapon. A gun with a mysterious outline, angled and boxy except for its smooth, molded grip, the twenty-inch-long P90. It was a smoky pink, like her clothes. This was P-chan the Third.

She grabbed it and slung it over her shoulder, thus completing her gearing-up process. With the familiar weight of the gun pulling on her, Llenn thought *I just don't want you to get busted up again.*

"Ooh! You got a new one, Llenn! It looks good on you!" cheered Fukaziroh behind her shoulder.

"Yeah, isn't it?!" Llenn was always happy to hear a compliment for P-chan. She spun around to see Fukaziroh in full battle mode.

Fukaziroh, too, had a very short and cute girl avatar. Her features, however, were so sharp they seemed likely to cut anyone who touched them. She had blond hair tied up in the back, with a knife holding it in place rather than a comb. This knife had also come in very handy when they needed it most in SJ2. Llenn and Fuka would have lost without it.

Her clothing and armaments were exactly the same as last time. This only made sense, as Fukaziroh hadn't actually been present in *GGO* between the end of SJ2 and mere minutes ago. All her items had been stored in Llenn's rental locker for the past three months.

On top of her brilliant golden hair was a green helmet that was just a bit too large for her head. Her combat gear featured a camo pattern that the American military called MultiCam. She wore a long-sleeve shirt and shorts, plus black tights and brown boots. It was quite a fashionable look.

Over her top she wore a green vest that contained bulletproof armor. It had some pouches sized to hold two-inch ammo grenades. She also wore a backpack that was positively stuffed with grenades.

Her primary weapon was the six-shot grenade launcher, the MGL-140. And not just one—she had a launcher for each hand.

These were monstrous guns capable of throwing lethally explosive bomb blasts thirty feet wide, up to a distance of a quarter of a mile. She made full use of it in SJ2, dispatching many enemies, even some she couldn't see when she unloaded the launchers on them.

Reunited with her favorite guns, Fukaziroh babbled, "Oh, my dear Rightony and Leftania… How have you been? Hang on, have you lost weight…? Was Llenn feeding you enough while I was gone? The entire time I was adventuring in the land of the fairies, I never forgot about you for a single seco…for more than a handful of seconds."

How warm were her beloved guns after three months of no use? As a matter of fact, Fukaziroh had one more gun. There was a 9 mm automatic pistol in a holster on her right thigh, a Smith & Wesson M&P.

But Fukaziroh was a terrible shot with a pistol. She absolutely sucked at it. In fact, she had fired it nearly point-blank at an enemy last time and didn't land a single hit. It made you wonder if there was any point to carrying it around.

I wish she would just leave it behind, Llenn thought, but she kept that to herself.

The other two people in the waiting area, Pitohui and M, arranged their own equipment.

M geared up in the same style as before. Toxic green-stippled camo covered his mountainous, burly frame. Over that he wore a bulletproof vest with pouches for ammo magazines.

On his head was a bush hat with a number of leafy bits of cloth that made its silhouette harder to discern. Over his shoulders was a camo backpack with the hugely powerful shield inside that had played a major role in SJ1 and SJ2.

SHINC's anti-tank rifle had hit the shield hard last time, breaking the joints that kept its eight plates together, but it had been restored, of course. Pitohui also used one of the shield parts manually for defense to excellent effect, so they had modified the shield to be easier to detach.

"Ooooh, how handy!" Llenn had exclaimed when she heard about it during the wait for Fukaziroh to show up. She might get the chance to use it, too, today. Not in an active sense, because it was so heavy, but perhaps if they were taking up a defensive position.

As always, M used the blocky M14 EBR. It had a high-magnification zooming scope that he could use for anything from sniping to run-and-gun combat. On his right thigh holster was the HK45 automatic pistol that he'd used on Llenn in SJ1. Lastly, there were four plasma grenades, which were more powerful than regular hand grenades. They would explode if struck by a bullet, so he kept them on the underside of his backpack behind him, as common sense dictated.

Pitohui's loadout was identical to what she used in SJ2, as well. When a player got to be on the level she was, they tended to find an ideal set of gear that didn't change often.

On her head she wore a set of black headgear, similar to those worn in sports, but with a more cybernetic look. It was lighter than a helmet but with good defensive plating here and there for protection.

Over her skintight navy bodysuit, she wore a bulletproof combat vest. It held a number of shotgun shells. There was also a ring of pouches for her main assault rifle's thirty-round magazines strung up sideways like armor plates.

That rifle was the KTR-09, which she'd used copiously against Llenn in SJ2. It was a custom model of the Russian AK-47, the most famous assault rifle in the world, with a seventy-five-round drum magazine attached for longer firing.

For sidearms, she kept two XDM .40-caliber pistols at her sides. On top of that, she had a very powerful alternate Remington M870 Breacher shotgun in its own sheath at her left side. Even more, there was a narrow knife in the side of either boot.

Lastly, hidden inside the fanny pouch behind her back, she had a single lightsword handle. The gun-world version of a sword, which she had used to kill a great many people in SJ2.

"Pito," Llenn said, approaching as she finished gearing up. The floating countdown said 04:33 now. There was plenty of time to talk. "You're starting off at full power this time. I thought you might wait to change halfway in, like the last one."

In SJ2, Pitohui only had her bodysuit on at the start. She went in totally unarmed for the challenge. When they fought in the mountain region, she actually stole the enemy's weapons as she went. Later, she sniped with an M107A1 antimateriel rifle that her courier teammate hauled around for her.

It wasn't until much later in the game that she put on her full loadout.

In preparation for SJ3, Llenn watched the video of SJ1 and SJ2 very closely. She memorized the guns and tactics used by the teams they had faced before. When she got to the scene of Pitohui's brutal battle in the waterfall canyon, she felt a cold trickle of sweat down her back—as well as relief that she was now watching her own teammate.

Pitohui answered, "Yeah, I guess. I wasn't able to prepare anything this time, so I don't really have room to mess around."

"Oh, I suppose that makes sense."

Llenn knew the story already. Pitohui's player, Elza Kanzaki, had been on a nationwide concert tour through just yesterday. She'd been traveling all over Japan, singing and singing and singing some more, giving encores until she practically needed extra oxygen to get through it all.

According to the online article she read earlier, last night's show in Tokyo, the tour finale, was quite a showstopping performance.

"So has it been a while since you played any *GGO*?" Llenn asked. She'd at least made a few dives since deciding to appear in SJ3, when she'd had time between classes. She'd tackled some tough monsters, earned more experience, and trained to get her edge back. Between that and her video practice, Llenn exhibited her hardworking personality.

But Fukaziroh interrupted to say, "Ooh! Yeah! I haven't played in forever!"

"I already know that," Llenn snapped, waiting for Pitohui to answer.

"That's right. It's been a while. I wanted to at least get one good dive in, but it just wasn't possible with the tour and all."

"I had to keep an eye on her," said M. "I knew that if she logged on to *GGO* even once, she wouldn't be back for hours. And she'd want to play again the next day."

"Ah, I can see that," said Llenn. Then something else occurred to her. "What about you, M?"

M's heavy jaw rose and fell, confirming what she suspected. If he was keeping watch over her in real life, Goushi wouldn't dare go into *GGO* on his own.

"It's been over two months for me, too," he said. "It almost feels nostalgic to be here."

"Hrmm...," Llenn grunted.

Out of the four of them, she was the only one who was definitely tougher than before. The other three were powerful to begin with, which was good, but it did leave them with something lacking in terms of teamwork.

Llenn had teamed up with all three at different times, so she would be fine, but there was still the question of how well Fukaziroh would be able to coordinate with Pitohui and M. They really should have found at least *one* occasion to hunt together, just to get used to each other. But it was too late to worry about that now.

"I'll admit, I'm still a little fatigued from yesterday, so I could have stood to hang out in the bar a little bit longer. I feel bad about putting on a poor performance. It's not fair to the audience—I mean, to the other combatants," Pitohui said gloomily.

"Ah...yeah, I get that," Llenn said, also gloomily. Then a sudden thought came to her. "Huh? Daaah! I was the one who said I didn't need to play, but you dragged me into this, Pito!" she piped up, little body exploding with indignation.

Pitohui looked unconcerned. "Oh, whatever. Look, I wanted to help you settle the score with the Amazons, you know?"

"Mmph!"

"No sulking now. Listen, I'll give you a nice present for being such a good girl!"

"Mmmm?"

Pitohui brought up her window with a wave of her left hand, and a metal box about the size of an encyclopedia appeared. Llenn grabbed it in both hands; it was quite heavy.

"What is this?"

"A present for you. Open it up!"

She put it on the ground and opened the hinged lid to peer inside. There were six two-inch grenades stored inside, resting neatly on a bed of heavy, shock-resistant molded pulp. They almost looked like a pack of eggs—only colored bright blue.

"Oh! Just like you promised, Pito!" exclaimed Fukaziroh, who crouched over the box excitedly.

"What? What promise?" Llenn wondered. Fukaziroh reached over with a slender hand to lift up a grenade and stare at it closely. It was the first time Llenn had seen a grenade with such a brilliant blue head.

"Mwa-hoh-hohhh! Nwe-heh-heh-heh!" Fukaziroh cackled. Llenn had never heard her do that before. It was unsettling. "Llenn! Do you know what this is?"

"It's a grenade for your guns, right?"

"Yes! But I'm referring to the payload! You know it?"

"Nuh-uh."

"Then listen up! This is a plasma warhead that blows up anything within a ten-yard radius when it explodes!"

"Holy—!" Llenn exclaimed.

She'd heard about them from the owner of the place where she bought the MGL-140s. 40 mm grenade launcher projectiles with plasma warheads—extremely expensive and rare due to their unfathomable power. They were as strong as the larger thrown plasma grenades, but these ones could be shot over a thousand feet with a launcher. In all honesty, it just wasn't fair.

Fukaziroh wished she had some of these in SJ2, but she ultimately gave up on them in favor of the pink smoke grenades that Llenn needed for tactical purposes.

"Six of them! Thank you, Pito! I love you!" she shouted, hopping back and forth like a child receiving a very good Christmas present.

I get it. Pitohui must have used her considerable finances to buy these for the sake of the team. Thank you, Pito, Llenn thought. Then another thought occurred to her.

"Hey, wait! That present's not for *me*!"

"Listen, Llenn. Don't sweat the little things, okay? You'll go bald early."

"I won't go bald at all!"

Fukaziroh, meanwhile, set down her MGL-140s and lowered her backpack to the ground so she could stick the lethal projectiles inside. "Whoo-hoo-hoo! One grenade, two grenades, three grenades…"

The main zippered portion of her backpack was already full of her ammo grenades, so she could only fit the plasmas into the side pocket.

"Is that safe there?" Llenn asked, worried. "They won't explode if you get shot in the back?"

Normal grenades were programmed not to explode if they got shot in combat, but the plasma types were different. This flaw had been introduced to counterbalance the overwhelming advantage of their sheer power.

If Fukaziroh got shot in the back, and the grenades went off, anyone standing within thirty feet of her would be caught in the blast and probably die, too.

She stopped in the midst of her packing and smirked. "Are you kidding? With three mighty warriors guarding my back? I ain't afraid in the least!"

"Fuka…," Llenn murmured, feeling a warmth in her heart.

"Besides, I don't want to die a lonely death. I would much rather have it be a huge disaster that gets everyone else involved."

Llenn promptly looked off into the distance. "Ah. Okay. So I'll make sure to keep my distance from you."

"That's so mean! I'm your partner! I'm your buddy! I came over here to *GGO* just to play with ya, remember?"

"And I'm looking forward to that. But it needs to be me who beats Boss at the end."

"Fine, fine, you can have her." Fukaziroh stood up, backpack straps over her shoulders. It was a very heavy pack, but thanks to Fukaziroh's ridiculously high strength numbers, she treated it like little more than a light jacket.

That completed the team's combat preparation. There were just eighty seconds of wait time remaining.

Pitohui said, "Shall we form up in a little circle before we head in? As a symbol of our special friendship!"

"Uh, isn't one of those friendships actually love?" Fukaziroh teased, referring to M.

But Pitohui immediately said, "No. I actually hate him."

"Yeah, that makes sense."

"Who wants a creepy stalker around?"

"I totally get it."

"I ruthlessly made fun of him for being fat, and then he goes and gets all thin and handsome all of a sudden."

"It's not even fair."

"Then he starts acquiring a fashion sense, and all of a sudden, other women are all over him."

"Simply unforgivable."

"I tried to beat him up to change the shape of his face, but it's surprisingly hardy."

"I just can't stand it."

"Instead, I try to mentally break him down within the game, but he just sticks around, takes a vacation to go practice shooting overseas, and gets more accurate than I am."

"It's like, read the room."

"I'd love to shoot him in the back at some point during this event."

"I'm willing to help."

"Please stop this!" Llenn interrupted, noticing how M was silent. "Look, you're going to make him cry!"

"Well, enough of that. Come on, everyone, hands in! Hands! Let's go!"

The three of them formed a circle with Pitohui and reached out to cover her outstretched hand.

"Here," said Llenn.

"Heya," said Fukaziroh.

"Hail," said M.

Pitohui cleared her throat. "Then I am humbly pleased to deliver a short message of encouragement! So, ah, Team Ell-Pee-Eff-Lem... Argh, it's so hard to say! Team! You ready?"

Yeah! They roared in acknowledgment.

"Not that we had time to prepare, but are you prepared for a bout of violent virtual killing?"

Yeah!

"Don't forget! One for all! And all for me!"

Yeah! ...What?

"Let's stick together! We may have been born separately! But I'll die as the last of us!"

Yeah......

"And since it's been a while, let's enjoy this game for the game it is! No outcome is allowed except for victory!"

Huh?

"All right, gang, let's kick—"

The time hit zero, cutting off Pitohui mid-sentence and teleporting them all away.

CHAPTER 3

SECT.5

It Was an Island. And Then...

CHAPTER 3
It Was an Island. And Then...

Llenn opened her eyes to see a shoreline.

The only things that filled her vision were majestic, roiling waves. They crashed heavily on fierce rocks about a hundred feet ahead. It looked like the Sea of Japan in winter.

The color of the water, whatever they would need to melt to get it this way, was a dull, poisonous-looking gray. The sky hanging above it was also gray, with a reddish tint.

The weather in SJ was poor once again. There was also wind blowing, at not inconsequential strength. It mostly buffeted her from the seaside, but every now and then it changed directions, just enough to stay uncertain.

"Ahhh…"

Llenn stood there, admiring the crashing waves like they belonged to some traditional *enka* ballad about loneliness, then turned away after a good five seconds. The land behind her was essentially flat and wide open. There was nothing but dirt ahead, without even any grass. The soil was dark brown.

In the distance, she could see a great number of little dot-like objects. They looked artificial, but they were too small for her to make them out at this range. As for what was beyond that, she couldn't even see. The land lost profile, eventually blurring into the same dull sky color.

Characters in VR games had excellent eyesight by default, so this was clearly designed to be indistinct on purpose. If visual range was defined as how far one could see through the atmosphere, then it was currently at about a mile and a quarter.

Right next to her, Pitohui called out happily, "All right, let's kill 'em!'"

Naturally, her teammates were teleported very close by. Llenn craned her neck and saw the other three right there.

M was peering through the scope of his M14 EBR, checking the land for any sign of enemies. *He's cautious, all right*, Llenn thought. There was no getting anything past him.

Fukaziroh, meanwhile, was throwing rocks into the ocean. *She's having fun, all right*, Llenn thought. She was not getting anything past anyone.

"Okay, people! Gather round and let's sit," Pitohui called out, like a teacher on a field trip. They followed her lead and got down on the ground.

The slaughter of SJ3 was about to begin. Upon teleporting onto the map, all teams were placed at least a kilometer apart, or about six-tenths of a mile. Even that was within range of large-caliber long-distance sniper rifles, so you couldn't be careless. It would be embarrassing if Llenn died right off the bat before she could actually fight Boss, her entire reason for entering.

It's been so long since I was in battle, my instincts are rusty, she realized, once she noticed that she'd been staring dully out at the sea.

"Bring up the map, M," Pitohui commanded.

In Squad Jam, the first ten minutes were always about getting your bearings before doing anything else. Some teams took the opportunity to just charge straight in, blasting away, but they did not last long. You had to cover the basics first.

"Roger that." M touched his Satellite Scan terminal and brought up a floating map hologram about three feet to a side. They could all look at the map on their own devices individually, but it was easier to do this with the holo-map when no enemies were around.

So this was to be their battlefield. The rules of the event stated that this would be an arena exactly ten kilometers to a side, around six miles, but nothing else would be known until you were within the map.

SJ1 had been in a place surrounded by unnatural, sheer obstacles.

SJ2 had been surrounded by castle walls on all sides.

And this time…

"I just knew it'd be an island," Pitohui said.

"What? Is this Bean Island? Is that why we're packed together in pods?" Fukaziroh joked, which everyone considerately ignored. Peas came in pods.

The map displayed a square island. There was no name written anywhere. *GGO* cut down one's hit points just for being in the water, so it was essentially impossible to cross the sea. Having a boat might make a difference, but surely none of those would be found on this map. In other words, the island was designed to offer no escape.

Llenn and her teammates examined the map closely. They needed to memorize the lay of the land as quickly and accurately as possible. Right after the start of the battle, the map displayed one's own location for a brief time. That meant the only lit dot on the hologram was them.

"Right on the southwest edge of the island," Pitohui said, pointing out the lower-left part of the map. The assumption was that north was always up on the map. For as close as the ocean was, it only made sense that they were right near the edge.

"Just like last time, it seems they've separated the powerhouse squads into the corners," M noted, which Llenn recognized. In SJ2, she and Fukaziroh were in the northwest corner, SHINC was in the southwest, MMTM was in the northeast, and Pitohui's team was in the southeast. Thanks to that, it had been quite a trek to finally cross paths with Pitohui.

"And we get to do it again…," she muttered, feeling that familiar sense of disappointment.

"Now, now, Llenn, that just means we shoot 'em all and crush 'em all and kill 'em all along the way, y'know? Capisce?"

"Fuka's right. When it comes to competition, you can't start by beating yourself. You must think of yourself as God's chosen unbeatable champion."

Her two companions had been through countless video game battles before. They had the right frame of mind for this.

"All right," Llenn said, getting her mind back into the game.

"Now, which way should we march?" Pitohui asked, pointing at the map. Her gloved finger started in the left corner and slid up to the right, toward a pattern there.

It looked like a bunch of long, thin lines, branching off and closing together. They spanned a forty-five-degree angle, from northwest to southeast. All told, the feature covered quite a lot of ground, over a mile wide and several miles long.

What the heck is it?

It probably corresponded to the dot-like objects Llenn saw initially, but she still couldn't tell what it actually was. It could have been city streets, but they were all totally straight, with no cross streets, which didn't make sense. Nobody would build roads like that.

"So…what is this?" she said. at last, not arriving at an answer on her own.

"Um, no idea," Fukaziroh said promptly. They might be able to glean more details if they zoomed in on the map, but M had the answer before that became necessary.

"It's a switchyard."

"Oh, duh! A swi-chard! I knew it… So what's that?" said Fukaziroh, who clearly didn't know. Llenn wasn't familiar, either. She looked to him pleadingly. *Tell us, Teacher!*

M explained, "It's a part of a railyard where trains and freight cars are switched around and sorted for their journey depending on the destination."

"Ohhh." "Ohhh." Llenn and Fukaziroh spoke in unison.

"The lines on the map are the many parallel tracks that branch apart for sorting. The dots you saw in the distance are the freight cars. Some of them are coupled, many are sitting on their own, and some have come off the tracks and tipped over.

"Ah, I see…"

Llenn suddenly recalled a time that she had gone fighting monsters in a similar place, with lots of train cars sitting around. With that mental image of a switchyard in mind, she asked M the most important question of all: "So this place will have pretty good vantage, right?"

"Depends on the number of cars, but it should be wide open for the most part. Not a place you want to take your time strolling through."

"I figured. But—," Llenn started to say.

Pitohui cut her off. "That's right. Given our starting position, we don't have a choice but to go through here."

She was right. The southwest part of the map was covered by the switchyard. If they were going to go anywhere else on the island, they'd need to cross a number of train tracks.

You don't have to put us all the way in the corner, you know! Is this supposed to be a handicap?! I hate you! Llenn thought.

"As for what's after that…" Pitohui pointed again. Above the switchyard, the north side of the island was covered by a grid pattern.

"Ohhh, I know this one! It's a city!" Fukaziroh said.

The mile or so of land along the north coast of the island was a developed town. There were some fairly tall buildings among the stretch, so it seemed like a fairly big city.

There were green parks and blue ponds visible among the street grid, but it seemed to be mostly urban. There were even thicker roads among them—highways? The north shoreline was straight across, but with docks and other port facilities that jutted out here and there.

"Hmmm," Llenn groaned.

A city was a battle environment that required technical skill and experience. There were many places to hide, and the range of battle tended to shorten considerably. You also had to keep an eye out for verticality, thanks to the great difference in height introduced by high-rise buildings. Danger lurked everywhere.

"Looks like we should get some very good urban combat here. Let's go clockwise, then," Pitohui said, circling her finger around to the east side of the island. That part looked green and fuzzy on the map, so Llenn could identify it at once.

"That's a forest."

If there were mountains, they'd have altitude contour lines—not to mention this was a three-dimensional hologram—so that meant this was an essentially flat forest.

Forests had poor visibility and poor terrain underfoot. They were unpleasant to fight in, too, for different reasons than the city.

"Let's continue. Below that in the southeast corner…"

The map depicted a great volume of something sprouting up out of the ground at intervals of a hundred feet or so. It looked like a swarm of giant mushrooms, but that obviously couldn't be the case.

So Fukaziroh was dead wrong when she said, "I got it! It's a field of giant mushrooms!"

"If it's a natural feature, it would be rocks, most likely. Overseas, I once saw some rocky outcroppings that had been worn down by wind and rain until they made towering formations. These were well over fifty feet tall," M said. He was probably right.

Ah, I see. Llenn used her imagination. The wasteland where the final battle of SJ1 happened was similar in concept, but the rocks there were much smaller, and she could easily climb up them. These ones, not so much.

So they'd determined that the map included a switchyard, a city, a forest, and giant rocks, leaving only the center of the island.

"Huh? What the hell is this?" Pitohui snarled, her finger paused in the middle. It was the rare sound of true confusion from her.

A grassy hill was depicted in the center of the map.

The pale-green hill climbed gently, the closer to the center of the island you went. It made sense that the highest elevation was in the center of the island, so that wasn't the strange part.

The peak of the hill couldn't be very tall. Perhaps 150 feet or less. Overall, it was a very flat map.

No, what drew Pitohui's skepticism was at the top of the hill, right smack in the center of the island. There was a rectangular space there colored black with the word UNKNOWN written on it.

"Huh? What the hell is this?" said Fukaziroh, echoing Pitohui.

"Unknown? So we don't know what's up there?" Llenn wondered.

"Oh, so that's what it means," said Fukaziroh, who almost certainly did not know what it meant.

This unrevealed area was about five hundred yards long and seventy yards wide, traveling directly north to south. Apparently, they wouldn't be allowed to know what was there until they saw it for themselves.

"Can the people who are nearby right now see it?" Fukaziroh wondered.

M said, "I assume they're intentionally hiding it, with mist or something like that. I suppose we could consider it a 'black box' of sorts. I would bet that they've all been placed at least a mile away from it."

"Ah, that makes sense. But if we get there, and it really is just one giant black box, I'm gonna be pissed! I'm gonna blast it with grenades!"

"Do you think *this* might be the special rule?" Llenn wondered.

Pitohui answered, "That could be it, or it might be something else. It gets announced when there are six to eight teams left, right? Until then, it's just a mystery to ponder."

"I see," Llenn said. There wasn't much point to worrying about it yet. It was still far off, anyway.

"Is everyone ready? Good." M turned off the map and went back to checking the horizon, just in case. Pitohui glanced at her wristwatch, and so did Llenn. It had just turned 12:05.

They'd wait here for another five minutes on high alert, check the initial Satellite Scan, then move carefully, taking enemy placement into account—or if they decided that was too dangerous, they would lie here in wait.

At least, if Llenn were the leader, that's what she would do. But the leader of the squad this time was M. Once they had agreed to enter Squad Jam, the topic turned to who should be the leader, and sensing that Llenn wasn't much in the mood, Pitohui settled the matter by executive decision.

What kind of tactics would M utilize? She'd follow the plan no matter what.

"Huh?! Whoa! Behind us, guys!" Fukaziroh yelped. It was rare to hear her so sincerely startled.

"Huh?" Llenn turned around in her crouch, toward the sea. "Dwaaaaaaah!"

It was a cry of true, unvarnished shock.

She couldn't believe her eyes. Even a few blinks didn't dispel what she was seeing.

"Huh? Wha—? Huhhhh?" she gaped, dumbfounded.

Before her eyes—the sea was rushing in.

The first time she looked, at the start of the game, the edge of the water had been a hundred feet away.

Now it was no more than thirty.

The waves were still choppy, but it was close enough that the spray might start reaching them. The sound was much louder, but they'd been too absorbed in the map to notice until now.

"Wh-wh-why?" Llenn stammered, but there was only one possible answer.

"Ha-ha-ha!" Pitohui burst out laughing. "Oh, no waaay! Ha-ha-ha! This map—this entire island—is sinking."

"Eugh!"

So it was true. That was the only possible answer.

Earlier, Llenn had wondered why there would be a switchyard on such a small island. There was no point to the yard if the tracks had nowhere to go.

She'd told herself, "Well, it is a video game terrain map, so I guess you just sort of accept that some things will seem unnatural," but now there seemed to actually be a proper reason behind it. This had once been part of a larger piece of land but was now sinking from some tectonic shift or other disaster, leaving only this island still above the waves.

"So the arena's only going to get smaller and smaller," Llenn said. Fukaziroh continued, "And the teams that survive will inevitably wind up in the center of the map…"

M added, "And it's a flat map by design, so we'd all ultimately arrive at the black box, I suppose."

My God! Llenn thought. She felt angry, in fact. That meant the powerhouse teams had the biggest disadvantage, being placed in the far corners! It was messed up.

But there was something about what Pitohui said that stuck in Llenn's head, so she turned and asked, "Pito, who were you talking about when you said, 'You're bad'?"

Pitohui grinned. "That should be obvious! I mean the novelist who sponsored the event! I'm sure that he must have suggested this idea."

"Ohhh, I get it now," Llenn said. She meant the same novelist who sponsored SJ1. The person who had sent so many signed books to rot in Llenn's closet. The one who was smirking and showing off for the camera on the program in the bar.

"After I beat him to the punch to pay for the last one, I bet he's pretty pissed, huh?"

"Ohhh, I get— Wait, whaaat? You were the sponsor of SJ2, Pito?" Llenn gaped, completely forgetting about the encroaching sea for the moment.

Nearby, Fukaziroh gaped, too. "Whaaaat? You *didn't* know?"

As the audience in the pub watched the live feed, eating and drinking and commenting freely and irresponsibly, a text scroll began running across the screen.

On monitors that didn't have any battle to display, they ran aerial footage of the various areas of the map, showing them off like some kind of travel program.

This island sinks automatically, the text read. *The pace of sinking will increase over time, until eventually, even the peak of the mountain at the center of the map will be submerged.*

"Whoa! Whoever designed that is *bad*, man!"

"That's terrible! Everyone on the outer edge is screwed!" the audience clamored, echoing Pitohui.

"But it does mean the powerhouse teams don't get an easy ride!"

"Bwa-ha-ha-ha!" Boss laughed. Before her eyes, the sea rushed in toward her corner location. "Very good! They really lit a fire under our asses this time, ladies! We've got to charge our way to safety—throw caution to the wind!"

"Ah, so that's what this is about," smirked the leader of MMTM. Before his eyes, the sea rushed in toward his corner location. "Very good! Let's make use of this, boys!"

"Whoa, whoa, wait! What is this?!" panicked the members of T-S. Before their eyes, the sea covered their feet at their corner location. "What are we supposed to do?! Hang on! This is messed up!"

"Well, that settles it. We'll just have to move a bit at a time," M said, getting up from a crouch. He peered through the scope of the M14 EBR at their surroundings.

If they waited in this spot another five minutes, they'd get a salty sea bath, so their only choice was to get moving.

"I'm worried about snipers, but with wind this strong, it's very unlikely that a first shot from a long distance will hit us," M wisely noted. If an enemy placed their finger on the trigger, a bullet line (or just a "line") would show you the trajectory of the bullet. That was a bit of system assistance to make the game more fun and exciting, and if your reflexes were good enough, you could dodge incoming bullets with pretty consistent success.

But to preserve the advantage of the ambush, the first shot coming from an unknown location would never create a bullet line. It would be a proper sneak attack and totally undodgeable.

The other system tool, for the benefit of the shooter, was the bullet circle, which told you the potential hit zone for the shot. A finger on the trigger summoned a green circle that only the shooter could see—and the bullet would land somewhere within that circle.

The circle's size was affected by the gun's specs, shooter's ability, distance, and other external factors, and it pulsed between its largest and smallest point in time with the beat of the shooter's heart. Of course, you wanted to fire when it was at its smallest, but that wasn't easy if you and the target were moving.

The effect of the wind was going to be greater than usual on aiming, too. The accuracy on long-distance sniping was going to drop precipitously. For now, they just had to trust that this would hold true as they moved across the map.

"Llenn will take point. Pito follows about twenty yards behind, with Fuka next to her. I'll bring up the rear," M said.

The point man was supposed to walk ahead of the team, scouting for enemies and occasionally drawing their fire. The rear guard was supposed to keep an eye on the territory behind the group.

So I get to start us off again, Llenn grumbled, but there wasn't a better option. She was the fastest and smallest target of the group. That profile made her the ideal person to take the lead.

"Got it. Hang on, I'll put on the poncho," she said, waving her left hand. Of the ponchos she kept in her inventory, the best one seemed like the MultiCam pattern that Fukaziroh was currently wearing. She moved her hand toward the button.

But then M said, "No, stay the way you are."

"Huh? But the pink will stand out," Llenn said, scarcely believing her ears.

"That's part of the plan," he said. Well, there was no arguing with that.

Skeptical, Llenn closed her window without the poncho and began walking. There was nothing but flat land before her. In the distance, the train cars were just dots.

While it was very unlikely that she'd get abruptly shot from a distance, the probability wasn't zero.

Ooooh, it's scary. Don't hit me, bullets. I hate snipers.

She walked onward, keenly aware of her fear, holding her P90 at the ready by her waist and being careful not to leave her squadmates behind.

After four nerve-rending minutes, M's voice said "All units stop. Stay low" in her ear, right as the alarm went off on the wristwatch on her left arm.

It was thirty seconds after 12:09. Thirty seconds remaining to the first Satellite Scan.

They'd moved forward a few hundred yards onto solid earth. They'd escaped the pursuing ocean waves for now.

There were no enemies on the way here or at this location. The switchyard cars were closer and larger, to where she could make out their shapes. Although "closer" still meant a thousand feet away to the closest car.

The wind was still blowing. At times, it got strong enough that she could hear it whistling.

Llenn dropped flat onto the ground to make as small of a target as she could, resting with the P90 sideways. Then again, the gun's effective range wasn't much more than two hundred yards, so she couldn't shoot at any distant enemies anyway.

The longer and heavier a gun, the farther it could shoot, and the lighter and more mobile, the shorter its range. That was one of those rules of gunfights that held true for the real world in addition to *GGO*.

"No enemies in sight. I'm the only one who needs to see the scan. Be ready to move at once."

He received a chorus of affirmative responses.

The first scan of Squad Jam Number Three was about to begin.

Every ten minutes, one of the satellite relics of the past would cross overhead. It would call up the location of the team leader and the team's name on the scan device's map.

The only ways to avoid being shown were to dive underwater and suffer damage or to take shelter in a large natural feature like a cavern.

The amount of time for the scan to finish changed every time. Sometimes it only took a few seconds, and sometimes it could take over a minute. It would tell you where your enemies were, but the inverse was also true.

For the first scan, you pretty much always had thirty teams still alive. It was like the bell ringing to let the fighters know they could begin.

"All right, it's time for the blood festival to begin. Let's bathe in that red stuff. I'm gonna blow up a bunch of people I don't have any problem with," ranted Fukaziroh.

"Don't kill all of them. I want a few, too," said Pitohui, equally bloodthirsty. Only in the video game, of course.

If only SHINC were the sole opponent to fight, Llenn wished.

12:10.

The scan started up.

But Llenn couldn't glance at her terminal map, so she had to trust M and wait for his report and instructions. Instead, she stayed on the ground, occasionally using her monocular to scan the vicinity. After about thirty impatient seconds, there was a sudden red flash in the distant sky.

"Huh?"

There was no sound, perhaps drowned out by the wind or just because it was too small. The shining red dot raced from the surface up into the sky in the distance, then stalled out and began to fall slowly, drifting in the wind.

"What the heck is that?" Fukaziroh wondered. Then there was another one. This one was much farther away than the first flash.

It appeared to be over the switchyard or maybe farther away. As hazy as the area was, it was hard to get a sense of distance, but the two glowing red lights were very clearly visible.

"Those are signal flares. With parachutes," Pitohui explained. But why were they fired? Who shot them up?

M had the answer to that.

"It's a signal to surround us."

The audience was waiting for the shooting to start now that the first scan was over. The sudden arrival of the signal flares was startling to them.

"Ohhh?"

"What's that?"

Flares weren't uncommon in *GGO*. Small flare tubes were quite cheap in stores. They were about the size of glow sticks and activated by pulling a string on the end, which shot them high into the air, where they deployed little parachutes that allowed them to hang and fall slowly for visibility.

There were other colors, too: yellow, blue, purple, and white, in addition to red. Newbie squadrons without the cash to buy audio comms could use them for communication, and they could also be used in place of illumination flares in night combat.

What they couldn't figure out was *why* the flares would go up now. It seemed like madness—who would alert other squads to their own location?

"What the hell are they doing?"

"Dunno..."

"Absolutely no idea," the crowd murmured.

Then one man shouted, "Ahhh, at last I can tell you!"

He wore green camo with a red beret. In fact, though no one else knew about it, he was the very man who had left the letter behind for the members of Team T-S.

Hey, you know that guy? the crowd mumbled in circular fashion. The man seemed pleased to have all that attention and launched into his speech.

"You see, that is the signal to converge upon a powerhouse team—to wipe them out!"

"Signal? What do you mean, M?" asked Llenn.

With his typical calm demeanor, M answered, "There were three teams surrounding the switchyard on the scan. All within half a mile to a mile or more. Two of the teams fired the flares. There can't be any meaning other than 'Let's take out LPFM.'"

"What?!"

"SJ2 taught us the importance of cooperation to eliminate powerful foes, didn't it? And there's no rule that says you can't make contact with other teams before the event starts!" the man in the beret continued to his captive audience. "So over the course of the morning, a number of participating squads gathered for a meeting and made a pact to work together to eliminate the toughest teams!"

The audience murmured and nodded to themselves.

"Of course, there was no guarantee that they would all be within range of one of those teams at the start. You'd need a way of getting in contact, but there's no way to use the comms to talk to other teams right away. So..."

"So they decided on signal flares. Once they learned the locations on the scan, they sent the signals to bunch up and attack as a group," Pitohui explained.

M nodded. "That's right. And they divided them by color. We're red."

"Not all the teams would be in on this, I'm sure. What are they thinking, I wonder?"

"We should assume the worst—that they're all together. Because..."

"Because I told them!" the man in the beret shouted. "I went to all the folks who looked like participating teams and secretly gave them a letter and signal flares! I told them that if they wanted in on the plan, they should memorize the colors and take part. Red is for LPFM, blue for MMTM, yellow for SHINC, and purple for T-S!"

"So you're sayin', because they found our location on the scan just now," Fukaziroh said, smirking happily, "that the teams nearby shot up their red flares, meaning there's two—"

Just then, a third flare went up. It, too, was red.

"I take that back! The three teams before us are one enemy! And they'll all come after us together! The mysteries are solved!"

"And there will be more of them coming over time," M said ominously.

Llenn turned back to face him before she realized what she was doing. She saw his massive form down on one knee, peering through the M14 EBR's scope. Pitohui had her own little monocular pressed to her right eye to help her scan the area.

Llenn thought about what she would do if she were the team leader. First, they could plan to fight back from the current position. There was no cover on the flat ground, so that might mean enlisting the help of M's shield and sniper rifle and Fukaziroh's grenade launchers, but if all three teams rushed them at once, would those be enough to fight them all off?

No, it wouldn't work. Even with M's shield, they'd be in danger if the enemy got to the sides or rear. They ought to fight in a place where they could narrow the attacks down to a single direction.

So where would that be?

If they hid behind the trains just ahead, there might be adequate cover. But even that wasn't going to be enough if it turned into an all-out assault from every direction.

Ideally, they'd be able to lure the enemy into a limited space, like Pitohui and M had done with the river ravine in the last Squad Jam, but there was nothing that convenient in sight.

"Wh-what should we do?" she asked, giving up and looking to the leader.

That same captain gave his decision immediately.

"Llenn—run."

"Huh?"

*   *   *

Twelve fifteen.

"Hyaaa!" Llenn shrieked as she ran.

"I'm gonna die, I'm gonna die, I'm gonna die! I'm dying! Dying! Dying! Eeeek, I'm dead!" She ran at a dead sprint. Her speed was astonishing.

Pitohui's utterly unconcerned voice came through a communication device into her left ear. "Oh, you're fine! Smaller body means smaller target."

"Yes. And if it should come to it, I will collect your bones to bury back home, Llenn!" said Fukaziroh's equally nonchalant voice.

"Hang in there," said M's voice, as calm and collected as ever.

"Ugh..."

Even faster than Llenn's sprinting speed through the switch-yard were the bullets that tore through the air overhead. All around her, red bullet lines that indicated the path of incoming shots wove and wandered like searchlights.

"If I die because of this, I'll curse you! I'll come back as a ghost and haunt you!"

"If you die in a game, can you really come back as a ghost?"

"I think I'm skeptical on that one, Pito."

"You're terrible! I'll curse you whether I die or not! If you

weren't on my team, I'd shoot you right on the spot!" Llenn swore as she ran, to keep from dying, to keep from getting shot—to keep surviving.

The moment she had finally cleared the reach of the bullet lines aiming at her from over her left shoulder, a new line appeared from the right, bullet whizzing past her along its course, right in front of her eyes and grazing her helmet.

"Aieeeee!"

And still, she ran.

Running as fast as she could was the safest option of all now.

"Doing good. You're completely drawing all of their attention. We're carrying out our actions in the meantime. Just hang in there a bit longer," said M, the only member of the team who treated her with any consideration. Still, the situation was bad for her.

Chweeng.

She heard the sound of a grazing bullet loud and clear, just behind her ear.

As she ran, Llenn screamed, "I knew I shouldn't have entered!"

But it was too late.

Four minutes earlier...

M's scheme was clear, simple—and cruel.

In so many words, it was a "have Llenn run around as a decoy, thus allowing the other members to escape" plan.

"Just run, Llenn. Right into the switchyard, then around inside of it. They'll focus on you. While you're doing that, we'll think of a counterplan and move to execute it."

"What? What'll happen to me?"

"Let's pray for the best."

No. Wait. Stop. She wished she could sit him down and lecture him for an hour.

But she couldn't argue against the team leader's orders. "Now go!"

"Dammit!"

She might not *want* to go, but she didn't have a better option. Running around, it would have to be.

Times like this were when having a reasonable, cooperative personality really came around to bite you.

As she raced at top speed toward it, the switchyard came into full, clear view.

It was an exhaustingly huge area—a wide, flat space covered in gravel and concrete, with so many parallel sets of rails that it felt foolish to try to count them, and many, many freight cars abandoned here and there.

GGO was developed by an American company, so the environmental design was essentially American in style. Both the switchyard and the cars found in it were of a massive size that you wouldn't ever see in Japan.

There were container cars with English letters on the side, tanker cars with black barrels on top, flat cars loaded up with logs, vehicle cars ferrying massive trucks, diesel locomotives with yellow paint peeling off, and so on.

She could even see the same cars scattered around, either a reuse of game assets or a natural occurrence.

There was a concrete tower several dozen yards tall, probably the switchyard control tower, toppled onto its side. The control room bulge at the very top had spectacularly flattened a cargo container below.

In the real world, places that had fallen out of human use almost always gave way to the spectacular rule of plants, but that was not the case here. Not a single blade of grass grew on the switchyard.

It wasn't rare to see ruins without any plants in GGO. And it wasn't because of the exorbitant cost of modeling and rendering all that complex flora—it was because the apocalyptic war that destroyed civilization had made the land barren of all plants. Supposedly.

"I'm almost at the switchyard, M. What now?" she asked

through the comm unit. She was hoping to hear him instruct her to find somewhere to hide.

Instead, he said, "Just run around the yard. Do it any way you can that helps you avoid their shots, but don't leave the area."

"Ugh! You've got to be kidding me!"

She plunged onward at top speed, right as a swarm of bullet lines appeared from her left.

"Enemy attack!"

Three minutes later, Llenn was still running.

Back and forth, across the switchyard. Left and right and left and right.

If she ran away from where the bullet lines were coming, next the enemy would be right in front of her. If she changed angles to avoid them, another group would be on a forward diagonal.

They were quite far away, as Llenn could only see brief glimpses of their silhouettes, but if they were any clearer, she would've already been shot dead by this point.

Up above, a new signal flare was rising into the sky and drifting with the powerful wind. That meant more teams had arrived to take part in the scheme. The sound of distant tom-tom gunfire had been constant for minutes. No need to wonder who they were shooting at—it was her.

At this point in time, Llenn was a cat in the wide open, being chased by people with nets. The cat was much faster and wasn't very likely to be hit by the "net" that was their gunfire, but more and more people were showing up, limiting her options for escape.

Llenn the cat had her own sharp teeth in the form of the P90, but she didn't have much room for fighting back. Her best defense was her speed. She had to keep running, not letting her concentration lapse for a single moment.

GGO avatars did not experience physical fatigue. Theoretically, you could keep up a full sprint forever, but mental exhaustion from a player's brain getting tired was a different matter. When nerves got fatigued after wild, extreme commands, they had a tendency to want to come to a stop, but this was a kind of torture that prevented her from doing even that.

Her only saving grace was the occasional train car. The hardy locomotives and freight cars carrying lumber would protect her from distant shots, so only when she darted behind them did she have a second or two of respite.

And then, sure enough, Llenn felt a numbness in her leg. "Ouch!" She jumped.

On the side of her boot was a red glowing line like a slash wound. It was the bullet-wound visual effect, signifying damage to her avatar.

The train engine was on wheels, so there was a space of a foot or more between the rails and the body of the vehicle. The bullet had hit her through that gap.

It wasn't a lucky shot from a spray of bullets, but the work of a good sniper, most likely. She hadn't heard a shot; they were using a sound suppressor.

Nope, can't stop—gonna get shot!

She hit the ground again running and checked on her hit-point bar in the upper-left corner of her vision. She'd lost hit points from that one. It was the first time she'd taken damage in SJ without at least firing a shot of her own.

As soon as she thought she had outrun the bullet lines reaching for her back, another red line appeared from the right without a sound and then another from the left. She was running out of directions to go.

"Aaaah! It's looking pretty bad now!" she wailed as she ran.

"Okay, come on back," said M at last.

"So close!" lamented the audience in the bar, all at once.

They'd been so looking forward to Llenn's inevitable demise, but once someone seemed to have her on the ropes, they couldn't help but root for the underdog. They were very selfish people, when you got down to it. All audiences are.

Llenn got shot in the leg and raced off with superhuman speed, which the aerial camera began following from above. It captured a nice wide angle like drone photography, beautifully vivid, causing everyone watching to briefly forget that they were watching a violent battle in progress.

It was a sniper from the one of the allied teams who shot Llenn's leg. In fact, it was caught directly on film.

He was dressed in the camo of an American marine, lying on the tracks, holding the marine's bolt action sniper rifle, the Remington M40A3. A suppressor was attached to the tip of the gun. He used his backpack as a stand for the barrel.

There were no other players around him. He was acting separately from the rest of his team. They were blazing their assault rifles with abandon whenever they caught sight of Llenn, which was only driving her farther away and helping her escape, in fact.

They had the advantage in numbers, and their target was incredibly fast and small, so he suggested that they get closer first for better aim when they attacked, but each of his teammates didn't care about anything but being the one to score the big kill—and didn't listen.

So without a better choice, he stayed put, trusting his gut that Llenn would pass through his field of vision again. He bided his time, waiting for his chance.

It was a gamble, knowing that if Llenn wound up behind him, she could very well shoot him in the ass without much of a struggle. However, he won that bet.

Chased by another team, Llenn wound up right back in front of him, as he expected she would. She was so fast that he couldn't really narrow down his aim while running, but as soon as he saw her stop behind the massive train engine, he took his shot.

The 7.62 mm bullet scraped along the ground—but it did not

succeed in puncturing Llenn's leg. Despite being from a range of only two hundred yards, a distance he almost always hit at, the bullet did not strike the middle of her leg. The bullet circle was larger than usual—an effect of the wind, no doubt.

If it had struck her leg dead center, the combination of short distance, slender leg, and 7.62 mm power might have torn it clean off.

If that happened, Llenn would suffer a lost-limb effect for about two minutes, leaving her only one leg to use. Then he could have called his friends over to make short work of her.

"Dammit!" the sniper screamed ruefully—up at the cloudy sky, rushing past with the force of the wind.

Llenn's good luck was still active in SJ3.

"Okay, come on back," M told her.

Her only possible follow-up was, "Um, wh-where to?"

She'd run and scrambled around too much. She had no idea where in the vast switchyard she was now. There were no obvious landmarks to distinguish the view, so she had no way of knowing which way she would find her teammates.

If only she could see the shore—but from her distance, it was still foggy, and she couldn't make out that far. She couldn't figure out directions, either, because the sky was cloudy enough that she couldn't make out the position of the sun. The tracks had been at close to a forty-five-degree angle on the map, so she knew they traveled from northwest to southeast, but which was which, she couldn't tell.

"Where am I now? I have no idea what my present location is, M! What address, what room number?!"

"You're fine, calm down. I'm going to fire a signal directly above our location. Run in that direction. Keep your eyes on the sky," M told her.

"A signal in the sky?" she repeated, dumbfounded.

She expected to see a signal flare of some color other than red, but if the wind blew it off course, that wouldn't make for a very good marker, would it? She kept running, her eyes darting this way and that overhead.

Ahead and to the right, there was a blue orb.

It was a blue sphere—like how the Earth looked from space—that suddenly appeared and shone high in the sky.

Then it vanished, just like a firework.

One, and two, and...

There was an ear-rattling bang. Once again, like a firework.

Llenn had counted from the moment of the flash to the arrival of the sound and gauged the delay to be about two seconds.

In normal atmospheric conditions, the speed of sound was about 1,125 feet a second, meaning that she was 2,250 feet away from the signal. It was also up in the air, which meant the place from which it was shot was closer to her.

This calculation was a trick that her eldest brother had taught her during a fireworks show when she was a kid. The smug look on his face when he guessed the distance to the fireworks discharge site flashed into her mind, over ten years after the fact, in the midst of a virtual world. How about that.

When the blast sounded, the bullet lines disappeared. Startled, the enemy teams had gone on the defensive, taking their fingers off their triggers and going into hiding.

"Did you see it? Run in that direction as fast as you can go. There are no enemies around us for the moment."

"I saw it! I got it!"

She changed direction as abruptly as a deflected pinball, heading for the direction that she saw the blue sphere. If the distance was under 2,250 feet, she should be able to clear it in less than a minute.

By coincidence, the angle took her directly along the tracks, which made it easier to follow. A toppled container car blocked her path along the way, but it was too much bother to go around it, so she jumped. "Hiyaaa!"

Her running speed was such that she bounded onto the upturned side of the car, ran a few steps along, then jumped even higher after that. "Yahoo!"

This was a game world. It was such a prodigious jump that if a gold coin had been floating in air, she would have caught it.

After crossing so much distance it almost seemed she was flying, Llenn landed on two feet in the gravel between train tracks and began running again. As she did so, something occurred to her.

That blue explosion had been a plasma grenade from one of Fukaziroh's grenade launchers. She must have shot it straight up, where M could snipe it from below to set it off.

Impressed at his incredible aim for such a dangerous stunt, Llenn also felt bad that they'd used one of those valuable grenades just for a signal. Still, it was better than her dying. She would have inevitably been surrounded, cornered, and shot to death otherwise.

On she ran.

There was not a single bullet line in her vicinity. It seemed that she had escaped the enemy's trap at last.

Finally, she had the peace of mind to check her wristwatch. It had just turned 12:19. Another scan would be starting in just one minute. She wanted to reunite with the team by then.

Thankfully, M seemed to read her mind. "I can see you from here, Llenn. Keep going straight," his voice said in her ear.

"Where?"

She stared around as she ran, but she couldn't see them. All she could see were the usual straight train tracks and the occasional freight car. She'd run across this area earlier; there were much fewer cars and engines on this side of the yard.

One black freight car rested up ahead of her. There wasn't anything else for maybe a thousand feet around. It just sat there, all alone, atop the tracks.

It looked about twenty yards long and ten feet tall and wide. It was just a big ol' square hunk of metal.

And it was from that box that Pitohui popped her head out and called, "Yoo-hoo, Llenn!"

"Hwuh?" Llenn had been assuming that it was just a box with a roof on top, like all the other cars.

"It's flat on the inside, so just jump over the side!" Pitohui told her, retracting her head, so Llenn obliged.

"Taaa!" She sprinted and launched into a tremendous jump several yards in front of the train car. With Olympic long-jump world-record-setting distance, she shot over the top of the car and inside.

As advertised, it was flat on the bottom. Llenn swung her sling-supported gun around her back. When her feet landed on the metal bottom, she leaned backward to slow her forward slide. She held up her hands to stop herself before she body-slammed the far end of the car.

"Bwoooh!" she exhaled, turning around. Across the car interior—was that the right word without a ceiling?—she saw her team-mates, looking hale and hearty. They had gathered at the front end of the car, antipicating that Llenn would soar safely over their heads that way.

"Nice Llennding!" Fukaziroh said, to save time.

"You did great out there." Pitohui beamed.

As for M, who gave her the reckless order to charge ahead in the first place, the only thing he said was "Let's transition to the next plan." He could have spared a word of praise or two.

But Llenn just walked over to them and asked, "What is this?"

It looked just like a flat, rectangular space trapped inside black iron walls. It was absolutely empty.

Fukaziroh replied, "We're inside an empty freight car. M found a nice one for us to use, and we snuck in here. We were able to do it because you were distracting all the other teams."

Aha.

So that was why she'd been turned into a decoy. And it was indeed the perfect place to hide in the wide-open switchyard, where enemies could strike from any direction. As long as nobody climbed up and peered inside, they would never be spotted.

But that just raised the next question.

"So what will hiding in here help us do next? Do we hide until they give up?"

Pitohui had the answer to that one. "Oh, that won't work. We've only got seconds until the scan."

"Huh?"

Llenn glanced at her wristwatch—she was right. She hadn't noticed the thirty-second warning buzz at all. M was already on standby, eyes on his terminal.

"Then they're going to find out right away! They're going to close in on us! Oh...I got it!" she said, struck with a sudden epiphany. "This car moves, doesn't it?! We can get away inside it, *chunka-chunka-chunka-chunk!*"

Any vehicle found in *GGO*, including Squad Jam, could be operated. In SJ1, hovercrafts and trucks had played a major part, and there were armored four-wheel-drive vehicles in SJ2.

If M could move this train car, they could just race along the tracks. That would be faster than human legs, so they should be able to break right out of the ambush. And if they could do that, it was a straight shot to SHINC.

That had to be the plan. That made sense. In fact, it was brilliant. One for the ages. *Bravo! Khorosho! Très bien!* Llenn gave him a mental round of applause.

Finally, M said, "We can't. The car alone has no engine. It won't move, and it's flat, so we can't push it over."

"Huh?" The mental applause abruptly stopped.

His eyes on the scan device, M reported, "There are more teams within a half mile of us now—five of them. Four more approaching from farther out. We'll ignore any other teams for now, but SHINC is still alive."

Llenn was grateful to know that SHINC was still doing well, but if there were now nine teams in their vicinity, that suggested their troubles were only just beginning.

"So if we can't move, and there are lots of enemies closing in... Huh? Then what do we do?" she asked in a daze.

"No worries! We're preparing now!" Pitohui said with a smile and wink so forceful Llenn could practically hear it.

CHAPTER 4　　SECT.4

The Great Freight Car Operation

CHAPTER 4
The Great Freight Car Operation

"They're close! Still within the switchyard!" barked the leader of the burnt-red-camo team as he watched his terminal.

This was the very team that had orchestrated the team-up to defeat Llenn in the dome last Squad Jam. He was still using the small AC-556F assault rifle. He seemed to like it quite a bit.

"It really worked out, Team Leader!" said one of his teammates, with the same camo and gun, a huge smile on his face.

"Yeah! You know what they say, third time's the charm! C'mon, let's go take down the toughest team in this game!"

The audience in the pub watched their screens, enraptured. There were other battles going on now, but *this* was the only one worth watching.

The results of the Satellite Scan appeared on their screens, too, so it was easy to grasp the situation. LPFM, considered the toughest of all groups in the event, was getting surrounded by an alliance of seven other squads.

A short distance away, the burnt-red-camo team met up with another. They were competitors, of course, and could've chosen to fight, but with a common enemy nearby, they weren't hostile to each other. Two more teams joined up, making a single united group of twenty-four soldiers.

Once they had LPFM's location from the scan, they hustled to spread sideways. The switchyard had few places to hide to begin with, and the attackers didn't even bother with them now.

Then another three teams caught up. That made seven in total, with forty-two soldiers. The patterns and gear of the alliance were truly diverse.

Naturally, none of those teams were SHINC, MMTM, or T-S. They couldn't have been there, in fact.

And if anyone in the audience knew the players present, they would see that neither Clarence nor Shirley was present. All of the players were men.

Forty-two was an incredible battalion. Even the combined group that Pitohui massacred in the mountains of SJ2 was only thirty-six strong.

"I dunno… I'm startin' to feel sorry for 'em…"

"Gotta rise above the bullying."

"You don't think the favorites are going down already, do you?"

Anticipation rose higher and higher among the audience. But there was one crucial piece of information that they were missing.

Because the live camera feed was not showing them how LPFM was huddling and hiding inside an empty freight car.

Just past 12:22.

"We're coming within firing range of the scan location!" said a voice among the line of players. There were no intra-team communication devices, so they had to use good old-fashioned shouting.

The forty-two players were slowly encroaching upon the coordinates that the Satellite Scan claimed was the location of LPFM just two minutes ago. They were less than nine hundred yards away. M could hit them with his M14 EBR at any point now.

All of them were already aware that he could shoot without a bullet line. But they proceeded without hiding anyway, because their strategy was predicated upon the idea that one, two, or even more people were acceptable losses.

If it was just one team of six, they might all get shot and killed before they closed the distance. But would that hold true for forty-two?

What's wrong? Why aren't you shooting? Do your worst! they felt, though they didn't demonstrate their boldness verbally.

Naturally, they didn't want their targets escaping around the sides, so the members at the far left and right wings used binoculars to keep a sharp eye out. Every now and then, calls went out like "Nothing wrong on the right!" or "No signs of escape on the left!" This was according to their plan.

If there was a freight car along the way, they first checked around it, then on top. Someone would hoist themselves up to examine the roof.

"Clear on top!"

"Anyone you can see from up there?"

"Nope, nothing."

"Good! Come on down."

Even with their overwhelming numbers, they stayed vigilant. The painful experience of SJ2 had taught them something. Some members of the group were the men whom Pitohui had blown up in that river. Some of those men had been shot in the dome by Llenn.

The one thing that unified their experience? "We got sloppy because there were so many of us."

So they stayed tight, didn't waste time with chatter, maintained constant vigilance, and crept forward slowly but surely.

And though they didn't realize it, they were within two hundred yards of the car in which LPFM were hiding.

It is a fact of life—both real life and virtual life—that a gun battle begins abruptly.

The sound of the first bullet fired instantly starts a merciless rapid drumbeat in most cases.

So no one would have anticipated that this one would kick off with Pitohui cheerfully calling out "Well, well, well, hello! How is everyone?"

When Pitohui popped her head over the lip of the freight car a hundred yards away and shouted "Well, well, well, hello! How is everyone?" not a single one of the forty-two men reacted in the proper way.

The proper reaction would have been to instantly start shooting at her head, but none of them did so. One of them was even polite enough to nod his head and say "Oh, hi."

"I'm doing great! So long!" she said, then ducked her head back down again.

"Huh?"

"What?"

There was a brief beat of confusion, until finally someone came back to their senses.

"It's that damn woman! Fiiiiiiire!"

And so the burst of shooting started.

Nearly forty men lifted their guns and began to fire, flattening themselves to the ground in anticipation of a counterattack or to stabilize their own aim, while some just stood in place.

A variety of battle implements—assault rifles, machine guns, submachine guns, sniper rifles—opened fire at maximum capacity. The racket was deafening. It overlapped so heavily that there was no way to tell which gun was firing from where. The empty cartridges glittered golden as they were ejected, falling to the ground and vanishing into little polygonal effects.

The bullets struck the black car, sending up huge showers of sparks. The way that the sparks bloomed from hundreds of shots made it look like a box of fireworks being fed into a campfire.

Almost as loud as the gunfire itself was the high-pitched sound of metal screeching against metal.

"And there it goes!"

"So that's where they were hiding!"

In the pub, the audience eagerly watched the screens. There were other battles happening elsewhere at this moment, but this was clearly the biggest draw.

A few seconds later, the sound of the firing diminished a little as the shooters burned through their initial magazines. Meanwhile, the men at the ends of the line began to slowly circle farther sideways. That was to keep from clumping up and making an easier target and also to surround the freight car better.

Flanking the enemy was the basis of a gunfight. *GGO* players with enough experience also knew you didn't form an entire circle, because then stray shots would hit your allies on the other side.

"They're way smarter this time."

"Your entire group getting slaughtered tends to teach you a lesson."

In the mountains and the dome of SJ2, they'd been too close together, which made it much easier to suffer damage as a group. They'd learned from that experience.

"But what was that chick doing there?" someone asked. The screen gave them the answer.

The men surrounding the train car unloaded on it with their guns, sending up another spray of sparks. And if there were that many sparks…

"Oh, I get it… They're not puncturing the metal."

It was evidence that the iron slabs that made up the sides of that car were extremely thick. The bullets all deflected off it, like an armored vehicle's tough hide.

"And that's why they took shelter inside it."

"Dammit! It's not working! The defense is too strong!"

The shooters themselves could tell that none of their bullets were puncturing the metal car. It was simple to ascertain when you saw the shining tracer rounds hit the can and deflect off on a diagonal.

"All units, cease fire!"

More and more calls to stop firing echoed down the line, until the spotty gunfire came to a stop.

With the devastating racket of the shooting giving way to abrupt silence, the sound of the wind filled the void, and the forty-two men finished fanning out around the freight car at a distance of about three to five hundred feet.

Some of them squatted or decided to lie down, but most stayed on their feet with their guns at the ready, prepared to shoot as soon as the enemy raised its face over the side again or to charge when needed.

The man in the burnt-red camo, who was also on his feet, peered at the car through binoculars. "Nobody shoot until you see their heads! We can't puncture the freight car! And they can't shoot us, either! So we're going to approach slowly! Once we're as close as we can be, I want everyone to throw grenades! Then we'll climb up the sides together and blast the interior!"

The men quickly realized that his orders were their best bet and the quickest way to get the job done. They called out acknowledgments with menacing force.

"Yeah!" "Got it!" "Uh-huh!" "Roger that!"

Fierce smiles adorned their features. Confident smiles that said *We're about to annihilate the favorites to win it all!*

The screens on the walls of the pub showed the men carefully approaching, guns at the ready.

The car was sitting all by its lonesome, with no cover or obstacles within two hundred yards of it to aid in a potential escape. If Pitohui or her other teammates tried to run away, they would easily get shot.

Not to mention that the snipers who had their sights trained on the edges of the car would open fire as soon as any of them popped their heads into view to make that escape.

The camera angle switched to an overhead view. Directly overhead, in fact.

Four players were visible within a rectangular space about seventy feet long and ten feet across. It was a wide-angle view to allow for visibility of the surrounding space, but it was easy to see who was inside.

There was Pitohui, who had popped her head out earlier, little pink Llenn, the grenade girl, and huge, bulky M. The entire team was hidden within the freight car.

And now they were being surrounded. Over forty figures crept closer and closer to the car along the edges of the screen. They were trapped like rats.

"Damn...you think they dug their own grave...?"

"Did they think they could hide well enough for it all to blow over?" the audience wondered, aghast.

But one person, at least, was more skeptical. "No, no, wait. That doesn't make sense! If they thought they were going to hide and wait, why did she pop her head out earlier?"

"That's a good point...but maybe the nerves and fear are going to their heads? I've heard people crack in battle all the time in real life."

"The chick who slaughtered all those people barehanded in SJ2? Suffering nerves and fear? You saw that battle in the log house, right? She's not the kind of person who freaks out and panics..."

He abruptly stopped, then murmured, "Log house..."

Two seconds later, he said, "I—I got it... It's...it's a trap. She... she popped her head out on purpose, to let them know where she was and force them to shoot..."

It was intriguing enough to capture the interest of some other viewers.

"What did you figure out? Tell us!"

"I could, but I bet we're about to see the slaughter happen much sooner than I could actually explain it," the man finished saying, right as the shooting started on the screen.

The men standing around the freight car began to topple over, left and right.

"There, see?"

*   *   *

Rewinding time just a bit, Llenn said "Hey, Pito, why are you sticking your face over—? Aaah!" just before a tremendous rattle of sound drowned her out.

The seventy-foot-long metal box was full of the sound of gunfire hitting the outsides: *ga-ga-ga-gan-gan-ga-gan-ga-gan-ga-ga-gan-ga-ga-ga-gan-ga-ga-ga-ga-ga-ga-gan-gan-gan-gan-ga-gan-ga-gan.*

GGO was a virtual game with virtual sensations, so there was no sound that would rupture the eardrums, but regardless, it felt as though she was wearing a metal bucket on her head that several people were whaling upon.

Ga-ga-ga-ga-ga-gan-ga-ga-ga-ga-ga-ga-gan-ga-ga-ga-ga-ga-gan-ga-gan-ga-gan-gan-gan-gan-gan-ga-ga-ga-ga-ga-ga-ga.

It was so loud that she felt that no one could hear anything she said anyway, so Llenn gave up on demanding answers from Pitohui and shrank into a ball.

Ga-ga-gan-gan-gan-gan-ga-ga-ga-ga-ga, gan-gan-ga-ga-ga, gan...gan.

The clatter finally died down after a few seconds, then abruptly stopped.

"Pito!" Llenn said, picking up where she left off, "Why did you stick your face out like that?!"

"Huh? What, didn't I tell you?"

"No, you didn't!"

"When you shoot first, every human being gets that dopamine rush of knowing 'I have the initiative,' which fills them with happiness and elation."

"Huh? Happiness and elation are the same thing! And?"

"So they get carried away and keep firing, and they completely forget about the trap they witnessed last time. As evidence of that, I present to you the fact that they're still approaching. See?"

Llenn stood up and saw it.

"......Ah. I see."

Then M said, "Let's do it. The signal will be when Llenn shoots."

Llenn pointed the muzzle of her P90 at an approaching man. When the bullet circle appeared over his upper half, she pulled the trigger.

Trarararatt, went the quick burst from what sounded like a submachine gun.

"Aguh?"

A man toppled backward, bright-red bullet-hole effects all over his torso and face.

One of the forty-two fell slowly onto the rails behind him.

Bing. A marker reading DEAD appeared over his body.

He was just over seventy-five meters from the freight car.

"Huh?"

The man who'd been just five meters behind him saw the whole thing happen before his eyes. *Why...?* He had no idea how his friend got shot.

It was unthinkable that the enemy would have leaned a gun over the top of the car and shot them. He'd been focused on the car the entire time, and their alliance's snipers were eagle-eyed on the lookout. The instant they tried anything, they would've been shot.

For a moment, he thought that maybe one of their so-called allied teams had shot him in the back. But the bullet effects were on the other player's front, so that was ruled out. He looked at the train car again.

Huh? Why?

Then he became aware that a number of red bullet lines were trained on him coming directly from the black box.

"Aaah! They're—"

But several bullets came promptly flying at him, erasing their lines as they went, and embedded into his head and throat, killing him before he could complete his message to the others.

*   *   *

The audience watching in the bar wasn't able to process what was happening at first, either. All they saw were the men surrounding the freight car toppling over left and right.

It was a very strange sight. Men who'd been so full of vigor and purpose moments ago, getting shot and dying just like *that*.

One man saw his companions collapse around him and turned to run, only for a glowing mark to appear on the back of his head. Dead on impact.

A man with an M16A2 assault rifle tried to fight back, shooting and producing sparks against the hull of the black car, but as soon as he'd emptied his thirty-round magazine, he was punctured with bullets in three places.

A man who'd dropped to the ground to make a smaller target huddled between sets of rails, holding up his MP5 submachine gun in front of his head as a shield. Bullets hit the gun, which withstood three of them but wrenched loose from his grasp on the fourth. The fifth put a hole in his head.

One by one, the number of DEAD tags around the black freight car grew. It was as though some dark aura exuding from the car was killing all those who approached it with black magic.

"There, see?"

"No, I can't see! What the hell is happening?!" shouted one of the audience members who was getting tired of the cryptic hints. Right on cue, the angle on the screen shifted.

Now it displayed the interior of the car. It was still an overhead shot, but much closer than before, so you could get a better idea of what was happening.

Llenn was in the center of the screen, which was focused on the left edge of the train car interior. She was crouching low, quickly exchanging a magazine for her P90.

The empty one dropped at her feet, and she pulled a fresh one out of her waist pouch and attached it to her gun. She pulled the lever to load the first bullet into the chamber.

Then she slowly straightened up and pressed the muzzle of the gun to the wall of the freight car. With the gun still in her right hand, Llenn leaned her face right up to the wall and, a few seconds later, started firing.

"Oh! I get it!"

"Me too! So that's it!"

"Of course! That's what they did!"

At last, it all added up for the bar audience. If they had just remembered it sooner, it would have been a very easy mystery to solve. It was the very same trick they'd seen Pitohui pull off in SJ2 before.

In other words...

"She's shooting through a hole they made!"

In the battle of the log house in SJ2, the full six-member team of MMTM had been proceeding down the hallway toward the room where only Pitohui and M remained alive. Somehow, shots came through a thick log wall that shouldn't have allowed any bullets to puncture through, instantly killing their member carrying a SCAR-L.

They immediately understood why: Pitohui had used a lightsword that could cut through anything.

"It's exactly the same as the last time! They hide in a place where you can't attack them, then poke a hole with the photon sword and attack through it!"

"Exactly."

Pitohui was firing her gun on the screens in the bar. The tip of her KTR-09 extended just a little ways out from the wall of the train car. She had her eye pressed to the wall, where there was another hole about its size offering her a view to aim by.

In real life, people couldn't hope to shoot very accurately under such circumstances, but this was virtual. The bullet circle appeared within the shooter's vision, and it didn't particularly care how you were holding the gun.

Pitohui was seeing a bullet circle that told her where the KTR-09 was going to shoot. She adjusted it to make sure it over-lapped a human target out there.

Blam, blam, blam.

Three quick semi-auto shots from the KTR-09.

On the monitor next to that one, the trio of shots appeared on a prone man's forehead and back. Pitohui hadn't wasted a single one of those shots.

"Well done!"

"Yeah, lady! Get 'em!"

The audience members who'd been rooting for the alliance of men just moments ago were now cheering her on in the same breath.

In the switchyard, however, the men went into a panic.

"Holy shit! Pull baaaack!" someone screamed—right before he died.

Little bullet-hole effects appeared on his head and body in suc-cession, meaning that he'd probably fallen victim to Llenn's P90. Compared to an assault rifle, the submachine gun did less dam-age per bullet, but over ten of the shots together would be enough to reduce his hit points to zero.

The surviving men began to run.

"Crap!"

"Yeep!"

"Gahh!"

It was frightening for them to expose their backs to the enemy, but staying put just made them easy targets. The black freight car was like the castle of some wicked demon lord, spewing deadly miasma. They had to get away from it as soon as possible.

At least let the guy next to me get shot instead, they prayed.

"Aagh!"

The unluckiest of them got shot in the back and fell, followed by more.

*   *   *

"Goddammit!"

One among them was a hero who refused to flee.

When he realized that there wasn't a single bullet line trained on his burnt-red-camo outfit at the moment, he decided to gamble. He charged straight for the freight car.

He raced as fast as he could go, nimbly side-stepping at different intervals. On the way, he tossed aside his assault rifle, the Israeli Galil ARM. Instead, he thrust a hand into a waist pouch and pulled out a grenade, using his off hand to pull the safety and whirling his arm back to throw it the remaining twenty yards.

"Gahk!"

The next moment, a 7.62 mm bullet without a bullet line pierced his forehead.

He had no idea that M's hole, which had been carved high into the train car's wall, was large enough to allow his scope to peer through it—and that he could snipe without needing the help of the bullet circle.

He still tensed his arm to follow through with the throw in the second or two he had until his hit points drained out, but the next bullet cruelly pierced that arm.

"Dammit!"

The hand grenade fell to the ground next to where he toppled forward just before it exploded. The blast only provided a light rocking to the freight car, its shrapnel clattering harmlessly off the sides.

"They're withdrawing. Shoot as many as you can," M commanded.

"Like I needed your instruction!" Pitohui snarked back. "Here we go!"

She peered through the hole with her right eye, adjusted her grip on the KTR-09, and fired again. One man went down, followed by another.

On the far side of the car, Llenn was shooting the men in the back, too. "Ugh, I feel kinda bad about doing this. Sorry about that."

She was using a "finger-burst" technique, leaving the P90's selector on full auto but tailoring the rate of her fire by pressing and releasing the trigger.

One of those unfortunate souls took the brunt of her hail of fire on his back and head and was eliminated from SJ3.

As the crowd in the pub suspected, it was Pitohui's lightblade and its hole-creating ability that had allowed the three of them to defeat a force of over forty surrounding them. In the time between Llenn's arrival and the enemy's approach, Pitohui dextrously fashioned the holes for them, just at the right standing height and no larger than the minimum size necessary.

When the initial hail of fire hit the freight car, they all went to lie down on the floor and even held the pieces of M's split shield over their backs and heads, just in case. While it was unlikely, there was always the chance that a bullet might enter one of the holes and ricochet around the interior of the car. As it happened, not a single one did.

Apparently, M had been in the practice of testing out shooting at various things he spotted in the wild to ascertain their potential defensive uses. That way, he would know if potential enemies could shoot through them—and if he could hide behind them in a pinch for shelter.

Naturally, he had done the same with the railway vehicles. According to his tests, any locomotive with a diesel engine was, of course, perfectly good defense. Container cars would let bullets right through, aside from the frame. Tank cars offered good defense if they were loaded, but nothing if they were empty.

And the roofless freight cars for hauling very heavy objects were extremely hardy.

So in fact, M had sought out this exact type of car for them to hide in. But they couldn't have the enemy spotting the group in the process of the search, so he needed a decoy to distract them.

Naturally, speedy little attention-drawing Llenn was perfect for the role.

Well, I suppose it was worth the cost of my peace of mind and a bit of my HP, she thought with a sigh as she eliminated yet another player from the event. She was being careful not to use up too much ammo in the process.

Behind her, Fukaziroh stared up at the lead-colored sky and gave them a half-hearted "You got this, guys. Good job…"

"Thirty down, in just seconds…," muttered one of the watchers from the crowd. His voice was a complex tapestry of emotion, from admiration to fear to annoyance to praise.

New to this iteration of the event were numbers on the live feed. In the bottom-right corner of the screen, it counted how many people had died in the currently unfolding battle. Indeed, it read thirty at the moment.

There had been such enormously fatal battles in SJ2 that this was a helpful guide for viewers to follow. It reassured players that the game developers were dedicated to being flexible and considerate to the spectating experience.

The camera on-screen switched to an aerial view that displayed many bodies strewn spectacularly around the black freight car with glowing DEAD signs hanging over them.

It was quite an abattoir. And needless to say, all the bodies were outside the car. There were no casualties inside. The slaughter had been very one-sided.

It was 12:26. The entire massacre of thirty players had happened in a little over two minutes.

"Damn, that team is brutal…"

"I mean, that's what you expect the favorites to do, right? But it's still not over yet."

"We're not done yet!" shouted a man in burnt-red camo from behind a locomotive. He was about two hundred yards from the black train car, standing directly behind a yellow diesel engine that was rusting all over.

It was completely off the tracks, and the wheels were embedded into the stone ground, so there was no concern about getting his feet shot off from here. It happened to be the closest bit of cover, so the men escaping from the horrible slaughter had rushed here for safety.

There were twelve of them. They were from a variety of teams—meaning that none of the allied teams escaped with all six alive. Some of them were the only survivors from their original squad.

None of the survivors were injured, but that was not a relief, just an ominous sign that every one of their comrades who got shot was now dead.

"Not done yet…? Dude, we're a wreck now… I'm the only one left on my team!"

"We really showed our asses there… She popped her head out as a trap, to get us thinking about shooting and surrounding them. And they did the whole shoot-outta-the-hole thing last time… Can't believe we didn't consider that."

"We just can't win."

A number of them were thoroughly deflated. They couldn't see any possible hope for recovery ahead.

But some warriors hadn't given up yet. One of them, a man in body armor and a green jumpsuit, pulled a signal flare out of his pocket and shot it up. It was red, of course.

The signal to gather more comrades rose into the leaden sky and began to float downward. The man who shot it cast the disposable handle aside and said, "We haven't lost until all of us are dead! Don't lose hope! They can't increase their numbers, but we can!"

He was right. Based on the scan earlier, there were at least two more teams in the vicinity. Optimistically, if they knew about the flares, there could be more reinforcements arriving within the next few minutes.

That wish apparently found the ears of the god of *Gun Gale Online*.

"Hey, y'all! We're coming your way! Don't shoot!" someone shouted from the distance. "Don't shoot us! We're getting closer!"

The voice got louder and louder, until eventually another team came into view around another vehicle.

"Yeaaah!" The twelve survivors were elated. Their hope was still alive—the cavalry had arrived.

"Over here! LPFM is hiding in that black freight car over there! They're shooting out of little holes! Don't give them a clear glimpse of you!" shouted a man in burnt-red camo.

"All right! We're fine! We can get to you!"

The players hurtled around the side of their train car and raced over. There were twelve in total—two teams, all men.

That made twenty-four allied soldiers, instantly doubling their strength. The men who'd been downcast at losing so many comrades couldn't have been happier now. They even exchanged warm handshakes with the new arrivals, when normally they would be deadly rivals.

The two new squads were quite distinct from each other. One had a civilian style with jeans and non-camo jackets, while the other wore matching desert coloring. But despite their visual difference, they were alike in their desire to take down a mighty foe right at the start.

"They're all in that car! They'll shoot right out of the holes they made! We can't get any closer because our weapons can't punch through the walls!" explained the man in the burnt-red camo, the leader of the survivors.

"All right," said the leader of the civilian team. "If only we'd caught up a bit sooner…"

"But at least it's not over yet. Let's give 'em hell!" said the leader of the desert-camo team, waving his hand to bring up the menu.

Before their eyes, a new weapon appeared and fit right into his hands. The other men's eyes lit up like children outside a toy store.

*   *   *

The crowd in the bar cheered at the sudden arrival, too.

"You can do this!"

It was a grenade launcher that the reinforcement in the desert camo brought forth. That was, of course, a gun that shot grenades very long distances. Because they were so powerful and thus rare, only a handful of players owned one.

The man's grenade launcher was the HK69A1 by Heckler & Koch. It was a break-action single-shot launcher with a contrasting round barrel and rectangular body. When the pipe stock was extended, it was about twenty-seven inches long.

It was a single shot, meaning that it couldn't fire consecutively the way Fukaziroh's MGL-140s did, but it used the same 40 mm low-velocity grenades.

"Land one inside the car, and you can wipe them out with one blast!"

The audience was right. Grenades exploded and sent their shrapnel flying all around, and they were especially deadly in an enclosed space.

If they could score one hit over the heads of the four inside the train car, they could pull off a stunning come-from-behind victory.

"Yeah! Get 'em!"

"We know you got this!"

"Destroy the favorites!"

Once again, the crowd in the bar had changed their preference for who should win.

"I'll shoot a couple from the tip of the locomotive. If any explode inside the car, rush them and clean up," the man said as he prepared the HK69A1.

He undid the lock, tilting the fat barrel forward as if it were bowing. Then he popped a grenade into the yawning hole, closed the barrel back into place, and cocked the hammer.

"You got this!" "Blow 'em up!" "We believe in you!" the others cheered.

He walked up to the end of the engine, got down on his belly, and crawled the last three feet to the edge. From there, he peered around the side and saw the black freight car.

There was the fear that a sniper's bullet might come roaring at him, but it turned out to be all right. Either they didn't know he was there, or the angle wasn't right to aim at him.

"Okay, we're good."

Behind him, one of his squadmates used a distance-measuring monocular—incidentally, the same that Llenn had—to spot for him. "Six hundred and fifty-three feet. Make it an even six sixty if you want to hit the back wall," he reported.

Grenade launchers shot in a parabolic arc, so hitting a target exactly from above required a very precise grasp of distance. The train car was only open on top. From this angle, it was perpendicular to them, so the projectile had to land within a range of about ten feet. Of course, a hit to the side might do damage to the steel wall, but that wasn't ideal.

"I want to finish them in one," the man muttered, pressed the stock to his shoulder, and placed his finger on the trigger. The special grenade-launcher bullet circle appeared, visible only to him. It was a green circle at a forty-five-degree diagonal. Its current location was about twenty yards in front of the freight car.

The HK69A1 had a metallic sight that stuck out at an angle, but there was no point in using it when the bullet circle was more accurate.

He lifted the HK69A1's wide muzzle higher and higher, pushing the bullet circle farther into the distance. He moved it very carefully, to keep it from drifting left or right, until it intersected perfectly with the train car.

Pomp. The 40 mm grenade shot out with a surprisingly cute sound.

"Got it!" the man shouted confidently. He was certain that it would land inside the open-roofed car. The little black dot flew through the air in a gentle parabola, passed its peak, and began to fall.

It plummeted directly down toward the car—and did not hit it.

The black smoke of its explosion expanded into the air about ten yards in front and twenty yards above the freight car. They heard the blast a split second later.

It had exploded in the air before it could hit its target.

"Wha...? Whyyyy?"

"They shot it down...," answered one of the audience members in the bar, but of course the shooter didn't hear it.

The crowd had a perfect view of the whole thing. They saw the grenade launch with perfect accuracy, arcing through the air.

And they saw Pitohui's smile as she cocked the M870 Breacher shotgun. She fired it only once. Over a hundred tiny pellets exploded from the muzzle of the shortened shotgun. In true shotgun fashion, they sprayed out in an array, lead projectiles like tiny silver dragées meant to hit birds and forest animals.

They blasted out of the short barrel of the shotgun like a net, expanding toward the grenade. The shot pellets struck the end of the grenade, activating its pressure sensor and causing it to explode.

"That's crazy!" yelled a middle-aged-looking player in the crowd. There was no way that even a shotgun could succeed at coincidentally hitting the grenade's fuse with those tiny pellets.

Then a voice from the adjacent table said coolly, "Sure, in real life." It belonged to a young man, but he sounded wise beyond his years. "Have you forgotten that we're in a game? In old-school first-person shooter games, it was typical for you to be able to shoot down cannonballs, missiles, and grenades with a regular gun. Some people could do it intentionally, and sometimes it happened by accident. Sometimes you had grenades clonk off of each other in midair."

"Seriously…?" asked the man who looked older than he actually was to the man who actually was much older than he looked.

"Absolutely. In fact, shooting down a thrown grenade in *GGO* is pretty easy to do. You don't need me to explain why, do you?"

"The bullet line…"

"Exactly. The big arc is drawn out in a line for you, so you just aim right for the spot where it's vanishing and fire. Very easy with a shotgun."

"Ah, I see… And she knew that might happen, which is why she carries around the Breacher…"

"Probably. It also depends on timing. That part is largely up to your own courage. You can't shoot too early or too late. She's probably practiced it a bunch of times—knowing that if she messes up, her avatar will get blown to smithereens."

"Ooooh, that actually worked. First time trying it, and I pulled it off. Way to go, me! Gotta give myself a hand on that one!" Pito-hui chattered, almost in the third person, as she ran her left hand down the fore grip of the M870 Breacher.

The empty shell popped out of the right side of the gun, so that a new one could be loaded. She didn't forget about the belt of shotgun shells draped down her chest.

"Well done, Pito!" cheered Fukaziroh as she raised an MGL-140. Leftania was hanging from her shoulder sling, so she had both hands aiming Rightony at the moment. She pointed it at the sky.

Naturally, if she fired it, the grenade would be landing outside the freight car. There was no way to see the circle at all. But Fukaziroh gently adjusted her aim anyway and yelled, "There we go!"

It was her first time firing upon the enemy in SJ3—a furious, merciless sequence of six consecutive grenades.

"How'd it go?" asked a man next to the locomotive, his face pointed toward the sky.

He was looking at a sniper who'd climbed the side of the train, poked his face the tiniest bit above the canopy, and surveyed the distant freight car. It was the man with the M40A3 who'd hit Llenn earlier.

If he said *Bullseye!* it would've been a sign to the rest of the twenty-plus men to charge in with their guns. But he did not.

"No good! It exploded in the air in front of the car! What the hell...? Did they shoot it down?" he wondered.

"Crap!"

"Well, just hit them with the next one. As long as you know where they are, the grenade-shooting part is easy."

"Yeah. We've still got plenty of chances," muttered the guy next to the engine, not seeming particularly concerned with the news.

"Huh? Doesn't that mean—?" noticed someone more clever than the others.

Just then, red lines silently descended from the sky—right in front of the men hiding behind the locomotive. Six of them.

Pom-pom-pom-pom-pom-pom.

A cute series of distant blasts.

"—Their grenades are coming over here next!"

If they could aim at us with grenade launchers, we could do the same to them. It was all quite straightforward.

Fukaziroh had been staring up at the sky throughout the battle, not because she was bored, or because she was engaging in photosynthesis, or because she was looking for dragonflies and butterflies.

It was because she was expecting that the enemy would have a grenade launcher and aim at them from above. M ordered her to alert Pitohui at once if she ever saw a bullet line coming down at them.

No line would appear from an enemy in an unknown location, but with the information from her teammates, Fukaziroh had enough of an idea of where they were. Thanks to seeing the bullet line, Pitohui was able to shoot the grenade down—but it also gave Fukaziroh the chance to learn exactly the direction and distance of the enemy.

The only thing left to do was mount a ruthless counterattack.

Fukaziroh fired six grenades in succession at the unseen enemy. She had a six-shooter grenade launcher. Was there any reason *not* to shoot them all? No, there wasn't.

The grenades swooped through the air and plummeted toward the locomotive.

"Get ou—!"

Boom.

The first exploded as it landed right on top of the engine. The blast and shrapnel assaulted the torso of the sniper up there, cutting him in half. Llenn's foot had been avenged.

Boom.

The second flew a bit farther and blew up in the midst of five men behind the locomotive preparing to charge. One grenade was all it took for the allies to be obliterated together.

Boom.

The third hit the back of a man who'd panicked after the first blast. His avatar shattered into tiny translucent shards, and they rained over his nearby teammates.

Boom.

The fourth burst next to the man reloading the HK69A1. He and his distance-measuring companion were knocked out of SJ3.

Boom.

The fifth luckily exploded on the top of the engine. No one suffered any damage.

Boom.

"Son of a bitch!"

The sixth and final grenade blew up just behind the man in burnt-red camo who'd been calling the shots for the group. The blast was so strong that it rammed him directly into the train engine.

*   *   *

"Awww…," moaned one of the bar patrons.

The six grenades exploded in succession, sprayed glowing-red damage effects everywhere. It had taken just three seconds from the first blast to the last one.

That span of time was enough for the space behind the locomotive to turn into Hell. It may have been computer graphics, but the explosion was a brutal, gory vision, the damage that such weapons inflicted on the human form.

Gray smoke surrounded the engine, obscuring everything.

The number zero in the corner of the screen jumped back up again.

"Was that all of them…?"

Ultimately, it displayed 10. That attack had killed ten, under half of the total twenty-four.

"Oh? That's fewer than I expected."

"Yeah. I figured that would be twenty, easy."

"But I bet a lot are injured, too."

The wind was blowing the smoke clear of the locomotive. The aerial camera caught sight of many men scattering like baby spiders to the breeze.

If they stayed there, more grenades might fall in. They needed to put distance between themselves and the enemy. That meant a quick retreat.

The men raced away from the train in a sprint. Once they were about a hundred yards away from it, there were other cars and engines around. At last, they stopped behind cover, looking for places to hide from bullets. There were no follow-up shots coming from the freight car.

Glowing damage effects were all over their bodies, indicating that they weren't in top condition. Many of them jammed emergency med kits into their necks as soon as they had the time.

It was now after 12:29. The third scan would be starting soon.

"The ones who just ran away don't really need to check it, I guess."

"Yeah. If they don't do something about the four set up inside the freight car, there's nowhere else for them to go."

"Couldn't those four just hang out in that train car until the very end of SJ3? I mean, they can wipe out anyone who tries to attack them. It's the perfect defensive fortress."

"Nah, they can't do that."

"Why not?"

"Why not? Dude...did you already forget?"

"Ahhh, this is really an ideal position. Wish we could stay here forever. But that's not gonna happen," Pitohui chattered from inside the freight car.

With her left hand, Llenn brought forth more ammo magazines from her inventory. She'd been shooting very economically, but the battles so far had already used up three (a hundred and fifty bullets), and she had nineteen left (nine hundred and fifty).

As she stuffed the new magazines into her now-empty pouch, she said, "That's right, Pito. Are you going to live in here until the end of SJ3?"

Llenn's reason for entering SJ3 was to fight against SHINC. Calling this picking on the weak would be a bit rude to the other teams, but they couldn't just hang back in an advantageous location the whole time.

"Aww, c'mon! Let's just live here! When you're here, you're home!" said Fukaziroh, who had just finished reloading her MGL-140.

But M had his Satellite Scanner out. "We can't."

"Why not?"

"How come?"

"Llenn, Fuka, have you forgotten?"

"Hmm?" "What?"

The two girls were equally confused. Pitohui just shrugged her shoulders in frustration.

"This place is going to be underwater before long."

CHAPTER 5

Clarence and Shirley

SECT.5

CHAPTER 5
Clarence and Shirley

12:30 PM.

Thirty minutes had already passed since the start of SJ3, and the third Satellite Scan was beginning.

"*Dwah!* I totally forgot about the ocean!" Fukaziroh yelped.

"So did I...," Llenn added.

"Hey, I wonder if this freight car will float. Maybe not, since we already bored a couple holes in it," commented Pitohui.

"Watch for more grenades, Fuka. The rest of us can check the map," M said. The four of them were waiting for the moment to arrive as they hid in the empty freight car.

Llenn jumped inside just before 12:20, so that meant they'd been fighting from that spot as a team for exactly ten minutes. It was good that they hadn't suffered any damage in that time, but they would need to move soon. The target, as always, was SHINC.

The third scan was the first that Llenn saw for herself. It began from the east end, the right side of the map. Bright-white dots and dull-gray dots appeared over the terrain of the map to indicate the location of surviving and eliminated teams. Touching a dot made the team's name appear below it.

She decided to ignore the dead teams. She knew that SHINC was still alive and in it, though there was no direct evidence of that.

But she was correct. In an area on the right that looked like a big rocky boulder growth, a dot labeled SHINC glowed brilliantly. Scattered around it were dead gray dots.

No surprise there! Llenn raved to herself.

The hardy women of SHINC had fought off the alliance of smaller teams that attempted to do to them what had just happened to LPFM. Llenn also tapped the dot right along the water's edge in a forest area to the upper right to confirm the presence of MMTM.

They, too, were surrounded by a number of gray dots. No doubt they'd been just as ruthless at dispatching their would-be attackers. You could really count on that team to put up a good fight.

But Llenn was too busy watching the map and praising her rivals to notice something.

"Ah-ha-ha-ha!"

Pitohui suddenly burst into laughter, and she wondered why. Pitohui was the type of person who *did* spontaneously laugh for no good reason, but if it happened in the middle of the scan, there was probably a reason for that. Or at least, Llenn hoped that was the case.

"Pito, what's up?" she asked.

"You'll see soon. Once the scan gets to us," she replied enigmatically.

Huh? What does that mean? Llenn wondered. She waited for it to get farther west to their own location. In just a few seconds, it was there, lighting up a dot just about in the center of the switchyard area.

She touched it, confirming that it belonged to them. So that told Llenn exactly where they were, but she also realized another, horrifying fact.

"Huh?"

When she saw the map just after the start of the event, the switchyard had covered quite a lot of ground across the southwest of the island. Even then, there had been a lot of space between the ends of the tracks and the ocean.

But now, that had been scraped away. In fact, part of the wide expanse of tracks was already intersecting with the shoreline.

In other words, the island was already that much smaller. They had covered a fair distance from the starting point, which was completely submerged by now.

On the northern edge of the map, over half the city was underwater. Some of the gray dots of dead teams were in the middle of the sea. Mysteriously, there was also a white dot over the water, indicating a living team, but that was surely because they'd been on top of a building and were now trapped there.

"The ocean…"

"Yeah, let's see, we've covered about a mile to a mile and a quarter."

"The ocean!" Llenn panicked, zooming in on their location.

That made it clear that the freight car they were hiding in now was only a few hundred yards from the southern shore. It was probably rushing closer even as she watched.

"Uh-oh, that's not good! We don't have inner tubes!"

Karen had taken swimming lessons with her siblings when she was small, but she'd never swam as Llenn, and it would obviously be impossible to swim with her gun and full gear on.

"Now, now, Llenn, calm down," Pitohui said, clearly enjoying Llenn's panic.

M said, calmly and rationally, "This area is flat and wide, so it's going to fill in slow and shallow. It's not going to cause much damage only coming up to our ankles. We just have to watch out for dips in the ground."

Fukaziroh stared at the distant sky. "Ah yes, that's no good. We can't stay here long. It's a shame to leave such a lovely home, with so much natural light… I suppose we'll have to move to higher ground," she lamented to a sun she couldn't see.

The enemy wasn't attacking for the moment, either because they were too busy checking out the scan or dealing with the onrushing sea, or because they didn't have anyone left with a grenade launcher.

THE 3rd SQUAD JAM
FIELD MAP

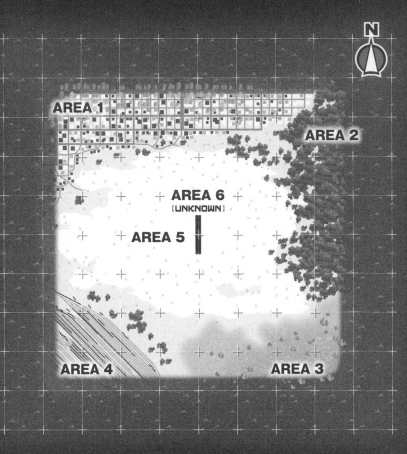

AREA 1

AREA 2

AREA 6
[UNKNOWN]

AREA 5

AREA 4

AREA 3

N

AREA 1 : City

AREA 2 : Forest

AREA 3 : Wasteland

AREA 4 : Switchyard

AREA 5 : Hill

AREA 6 : Unknown

The scan was about to wrap up. At the very end, Llenn looked around their vicinity for more foes. They were so close the dots were practically stuck together, but at least she could get a direction. The teams Fukaziroh's grenade bombardment damaged earlier were now to the northeast.

They'd moved a bit farther away, and there were one, two, three…six teams still alive. She could assume that few if any were still at full health, but there was no point in being sloppy. They didn't know yet if they were dealing with just six players or a full thirty-six.

There was also another team moving toward the bunch from the north at the time the scan finished. It was 12:31.

"Okay, M. Give us orders," Pitohui demanded of the team leader. She wasn't coming up with any plans of her own. Llenn couldn't tell if that was out of respect for their leader, or as a test, or both, or if she just didn't want to bother using her brain.

M placed the terminal back in his pocket, picked up the backpack with the shield inside from its spot at his feet, and easily hauled it over his shoulder. "Prepare to move out."

"Okeydoke. Where to?" Pitohui placed her KTR-09 in a sling. She was going to need both hands to get out of here first.

"Northeast. We're plunging straight through where the enemies are now."

"We are?" Llenn said, not sure if she'd misheard, or if she was right, and M was just losing it.

But M, as always, was just being M. "If we run east or north and get blocked off by the water, we're done for. Instead, let's choose what gives us the best chance at survival. If the other teams get in our way, we've got the skill to deal with them."

"Ugh…"

He was right, and she understood why, but she wasn't really into the idea. Not at all. She couldn't help but grumble about it.

"Yep, that sounds best. Let's do it," Fukaziroh agreed easily. She lifted an MGL-140 in each hand, wrapping up her prep period.

"All right, fine…" Llenn gave up. There wasn't any other way to do it. And in that case, there was no use wasting time. "Let's hurry!" she told her teammates.

"No, wait," said M, to her disbelief. "Not quite yet. We're going to wait for when the waves hit this spot."

The fourteen players hiding behind the other engines and cars were just as panicked about the ocean rushing in on them from what they saw on the scan map. It was especially alarming to the players who'd traveled outward from the center of the map, as they didn't realize the island was in the process of sinking.

"Wha—?! I don't believe it! We gotta get outta here!"

"Yeah… Fortunately, if we're gonna run away from *them*, it'll take us closer to the center."

"I don't want to drown."

Some of the players were more inclined to run for safety, while others yearned for a chance to avenge their fallen squadmates.

"But if we run now, then the whole point of teaming up to take out one of the powerhouses will be lost. We ought to make beating Ell-Pee-Elf…argh! Beating Pitohui's team should be our top priority. Let's keep them stuck in place so they drown."

"I'm fine with working together against them. But what's the point of going down with them? It just makes things easier for the surviving teams after us."

"Wait, wait. How will we fight when we're recovering?"

That player was right. Several of them were still significantly damaged from Fukaziroh's bombardment. They'd taken their med kit shots and were in the process of healing, of course, but they needed another two minutes for it to finish—even longer, for those who were gravely wounded.

"We can't fight at full strength yet. What do we do if they start charging this way to avoid the ocean?"

"We shoot back! Lying in wait obviously gives us an advantage!"

"But they've got that speedy little girl, the grenade launchers, a genius sniper, and…"

"Why would you assume we'll lose before you even try?! We still have the advantage in numbers!"

"Hey, dumbass, if that was all that mattered, we would have won earlier… C'mon, use your brain."

"What, do you have some brilliant plan, then?!"

"I'm saying, we have to think about it! You *do* have a brain, don't you?"

"What'd you say?!"

They got progressively more heated, sniping back and forth under the pressure. Then came a voice from the distance. "Excuse me! May we join you? We saw the red signal flare!"

"Oh? You heard that?"

"Yeah!"

"Great! You're in!"

"Those must be the folks who were nearby on the scan!"

The alliance of fourteen set aside their ugly squabbling for the moment and rejoiced. Nothing like reinforcements to improve one's mood.

"Over here, guys! Stay in cover behind the cars, so you don't get shot from the southwest!"

"Got it! And don't you shoot us, either!"

The men felt slightly better about their chances, believing that they were getting another six comrades. After a wait of about thirty seconds, they heard footsteps over gravel, and then their reinforcements arrived from underneath one of the train cars.

"Hiya! We'll join you!" said a very handsome and breezy fellow who could have come out of a boy band. He wore all-black combat gear, top and bottom, and an equipment vest. Large, long magazine pouches lined his stomach.

His weapon was the AR-57, a weird chimera of the M16 and P90. In a holster on his right was the FN Five-Seven pistol. Both guns used the same bullets. A pouch on his left side held four hand grenades.

"Hiya…"

And there was also a tanned man in camo carrying an FA-MAS assault rifle. It was a French gun in the bullpup style, meaning that the magazine was loaded behind the grip and trigger.

That made the gun shorter overall and easier to control when firing bursts, so it was popular to use in *GGO*. The gun's caliber was 5.56 mm, same as the M16. It was often nicknamed The Trumpet for its appearance.

The two sidled over to the fourteen and crouched. The handsome one smiled and said, "I'm Clarence. This is my teammate, Sam. We were also in SJ2, but this is probably the first time we've met any of you. A pleasure!"

"Thanks for coming! It's…just the two of you?" they asked—an obvious question.

"Unfortunately!" Clarence answered. "But we'll work hard for the cause!"

"Who got you? One of the distant powerhouse teams? Or did you get into a fight with some other random group?"

"Huh? No, it's just the two of us. No one else could get the time off."

"Oh…"

"Hey, you don't have to look so disappointed! We're gonna do our very best! Just fill us in on the situation!" Clarence exclaimed with a dazzling smile.

"…"

Sam never said a word.

The audience in the pub saw the arrival of Clarence and Sam—and the subsequent sitrep to bring them up to speed.

"Oh! That's the guy who got beat up by Llenn in the dome last time and gave her all the ammo."

"Ahhh, yeah, the handsome one. And that gift ended up saving Llenn," recalled some of the audience members.

"If they're just arriving now, they must've come from a long way away. Is he gonna fight Llenn for sure this time?"

"A revenge match! How exciting!"

Others were more excited to root for him. They did not realize that they were really rooting for *her.*

"I see… Wow, what a horrible map this time. I don't want to drown," was Clarence's first reaction to the news. "But we've still got the advantage, right? We're totally in this still!" she added with a refreshing smile.

Naturally, the men asked, "But how?"

"The space between the train cars around here is flat and has no cover, right? We'll have plenty of chances to shoot at them. And there's only four of them."

"Yeah, we know. But they're not four typical players."

"True, but if you don't mind me giving you some painful advice, you're not making use of your numerical superiority. You were around the side of a train engine earlier? Why were you all in one place? I would have split us up into pairs and set up a net just within visible range of the black freight car. Then I wouldn't move. The enemy has to move to get away from the waves, so you shoot them when they do. And if they start to push you aside, fall back and let the other teams attack from the sides," Clarence said with great confidence.

The fourteen men seemed impressed. "Oh, yeah, I suppose."

"That might work."

They'd been so wrapped up in discussion over their mindset that they hadn't come up with any tactical plans, so having a workable strategy was like a ray of hope and possibility shining through the gloom.

"Okay! It's too early to give up!"

"Let's go with that plan!"

"Yeah! And we can continue healing hit points while we're waiting!"

As more of them offered encouragement for the plan, the group's morale shot up. That was the old group mentality, for better or for worse.

"We're gonna go with your plan, Clarence!"

"Yeah, go right ahead! I'm glad to hear it! Let us join you!"

And so the sixteen men—make that fifteen men and one woman—became one to defeat their powerful enemies.

Or at least, so it seemed.

"…"

There was one player who watched it happen through the round viewer of a pair of binoculars.

It was 12:35.

There had been a long period of following the switchyard without any battle or gunfire.

"So…what's happening now…?"

The audience wasn't bothered with any of the other battles going on. They awaited further developments here with bated breath.

On one of the screens, Team LPFM was shown inside of the train car. The four of them had been waiting in place ever since the last scan. The ocean was rushing up on their position.

Earlier, the camera had to be very high up to have a wide enough angle to capture both the freight car and the edge of the water, but now it was much closer. The sea was within a hundred yards of them.

Like floodwaters, the ocean crept up closer and closer. It was eerie without any waves, but because of the way the island was flooding, the "shore" was very shallow and long, so the waves were breaking long before they reached this point.

The team was aware that the water was approaching, of course. M got up several times and peered through the hole in the side wall to check on its status.

Another screen followed the state of the ambushers. The sixteen-member alliance, after the arrival of Clarence, had split into teams of two or three and spread out north and east of the black freight car. The cameras had been following them sneaking around.

Now each clump of them was hiding behind a group of cars, waiting for LPFM to emerge. The density of cars was loose, so their fan of coverage came at intervals of thirty to fifty yards. In the Warring States period of Japanese history, this was known as the "crane's wing" formation, for its resemblance to the wide wingspan of those great birds.

There was about five hundred yards of space between them and the black freight car where LPFM lurked. That was more distance than the maximum range of Fukaziroh's grenade launchers, with a few train cars to spare.

It was a stalemate.

It looked disadvantageous to LPFM, who were being approached by the sea to the south and west—and whose one way out to the northeast was blocked by enemies waiting for them.

"It looks bad for them...but LPFM's tough, you know? Wouldn't they just be able to force their way through a siege this shallow? Once they know where the ambush is, they can snipe and grenade 'em there, right?" said someone who knew the four of them had more sheer power than the others.

"But I do think this strategy of their enemies is going to work better than the last one. The difference in numbers is big. And the battlefield is flat and open. If they're charging ahead and get shot from the flanks, big slow M is going down first, don't you think? If one person dies, that's a game changer, and it'll push momentum away from them," said another, who believed that the number of people and guns would prove decisive.

Wherever they fell on this spectrum of expectations, all the bar patrons had the same thought.

When will this fight start already? We wanna see the four-man favorites vs. the alliance of sheer numbers!

So they all watched the inert screens, attention focused, not wanting to miss a single moment of it.

* * *

And then, at 12:36, there was movement.

Four people left the black freight car as the seawater approached. A pink shrimp, a blond shrimp, a woman in black, and a huge man in camo.

"There they go!"

One of the people watching through a monocular from the roof of an engine promptly shot up a red signal flare to warn the others.

As soon as the red light rose into the leaden sky, there was a high-pitched gunshot, and the final battle of the switchyard had begun at last.

"Huuuuuh?"

"What was thaaat?"

"Excuse meeeee?" screeched the audience in the pub, bolting to their feet.

When treated to a tremendous shock, human beings tend to react one of two ways: to shout or to go silent.

"……"

Some of the audience paused with their half-drunk glasses in the air, unable to move.

In either case, the two sides were united in disbelief.

On the screen, the men surrounding LPFM in their siege formation were getting shot left and right.

In the back.

"Bwa-ha-ha-ha! This is fuuun!"

The AR-57 on Clarence's right shoulder spat gunfire in a bright and energetic rhythm.

Like Llenn's P90, it took advantage of a very high firing rate to emit a punchy snare drumroll of percussion. The empty cartridges shot downward out of the hole where the M16 would accept its magazine and bounced off of metal tracks and ties before they vanished.

Clarence was shooting at enemies within her sight. Just thirty feet away, in fact.

"Wait— Stop— You idio— Don't—," her victim shouted, waving his hands at her.

Clarence poured bullets into the man's face without mercy or hesitation, only stopping when he was properly dead. Two bodies lay next to the wheel of the train car.

"And that's one down! I mean, two in one down!" Clarence crowed, switching out another forty-round magazine. She still had ten rounds to go, but she switched it out anyway.

Then Sam, who was crouched behind her with smoke wafting from the barrel of the FA-MAS, offered a heartfelt "I'm sorry…"

The audience in the pub saw everything.

First, the red signal flare went up, then Clarence and Sam left their position on the far-right wing of the formation. They sprinted over to the adjacent group hiding behind a different car and, without warning or mercy, opened fire on them.

Once they'd killed them, Clarence and Sam began to switch out their ammo. When they were done, Clarence practically skipped along to the freight car next to that one. Sam followed behind her.

There were two more players there. They were just in the middle of affirming their excitement to shoot, having seen the signal that indicated LPFM had emerged from hiding.

"Oh, they don't get it…," someone in the crowd said. The men had no idea that a source of childish, mirthful murder was approaching them.

Clarence and Sam popped out from behind the car, AR-57 and FA-MAS firing in unison, spraying a hail of bullets onto their hapless victims. No character could survive full auto fire from two guns, from only twenty yards away, and at a rear angle.

Helpless, the men died and dropped out of SJ3, glowing bullet-wound effects on their faces and bodies. They probably never even knew who had shot them.

"Wha—?! What's up with them?! They just shot people on their own side!" screamed a man in a beret, spittle flying from his lips.

Indeed, this was the very person who had secretly gone to all those teams to propose his plan for joining forces to defeat the toughest squads of all. He had, of course, passed a letter and some signal flares to Clarence and Sam's team. Which was why he was so shocked that they would suddenly start firing on the other allied squads.

"I mean, they're *not* on the same side," someone else more rational said to the man in the beret, who was red-faced to the point of being purple.

"What?!"

"This is a battle royale. You can team up or split apart as you please. You can shoot your own teammates dead in this game, so why would anyone complain about shooting other teams that are your enemies from the start?"

"……"

The man in the beret scrunched up his face, unable to argue against that point.

To settle the matter, someone else then added, "Well, at least things are getting interesting!"

"This is exciting, huh, Sam?!"

"Uh, whatever you say!" Sam replied, practically in tears, as Clarence raced happily onward to the next target.

They burst past the next car, changed directions, and saw two men looking back at them. These ones were only twenty yards away. They were on alert due to the gunshots behind them, however. The famed Cold War muzzles of the M4A1 and AK-47 turned to the visitors, along with four suspicious eyes.

"Eep!" Sam shrieked, right as Clarence shouted, "Enemies to our flanks! They were waiting to ambush us! Already got four of us, and they're catching up soon! Give us some backup!"

"..."

Sam just gave her a side-eye at the shameless lies from his teammate's mouth.

"What...? Shit!"

"Which way are they coming from?!"

The two men took Clarence's lie at face value, failing to parse the situation. The M4A1 and AK-47 drifted away from Clarence and Sam toward the freight car they'd just run around.

"From right here!" Clarence said as soon as the bullet lines stopped pointing at her. She opened fire with the AR-57 at ultra-close range.

"Gwah!"

The man with the AK-47 didn't give up until the end, despite being riddled with bullets. He shifted to the left, trying to shield his comrade. Then he died from his wounds.

The man with the M4A1 didn't get shot in the head or torso thanks to his teammate, but a bullet did go through his right arm, and the shock and numbness of it caused him to drop his weapon. "Gah!"

The M4A1 clattered loudly to the rails below. He scrambled to grab it with his left hand, but Clarence stomped down on the weapon first. "There we go!"

He looked up into Clarence's handsome features and winning smile.

"Why did you betray us...?"

Bang.

Clarence shot him in the head.

"I dunno, it just seemed more fun this way!" she proclaimed with a grin.

*   *   *

Clarence and Sam had dispatched six of the original fourteen, and they weren't done yet.

"I suppose they've figured it out by now, right? I mean, they're not idiots."

She was hiding on the west side of a freight car, switching out her magazine again.

"What are we doing now? What's going to happen to us?" Sam wailed from behind her.

"Good question. No answers," she said happily, without turning around. "You know, I've always wanted to perform one really huge act of betrayal."

"So are you satisfied? Let's get out of here, then! If we wait around too long, LPFM will show up!"

"Yeah, that's probably the best idea, because we can't beat them, but…it's also no fun."

"Dahhh! I can't put up with this anymore! Forget it, I'm running away!"

"C'mon, don't be that way. Just a bit longer. It'll be tough on your own, don't you see?"

"Why would I care about—?"

Buh-pamm.

Sam abruptly stopped speaking, drowned out by a muffled explosion.

"Hmm?" Clarence turned around to see Sam standing there with a glowing bullet effect on his chest.

"Wha…?" Sam had no idea what had happened and couldn't see it for himself.

But Clarence could see the brilliant-red glow across his entire chest very clearly. Bullet holes in *GGO* were small as a general rule, usually no bigger than a clenched fist in size—but the damage across Sam's chest was so wide, he might as well have been smacked with a log.

Sam's body toppled slowly backward.

"Oh, crap!" Clarence ducked down next to him, where the DEAD tag had lit up, hovering over the body.

Byeum.

A bullet rocketed through the air where Clarence's chest had just been, thudding into the gravel just a few yards away.

Bam! The rock there practically exploded into pieces. The sniper's bullet had gone from north to south.

"Eek! So scary!" Clarence screamed, though with great delight.

"Huh? What the hell just…? Huh?"

The audience in the bar had a good view of it all. One of the two traitors had gotten shot, his chest lit up red. And the other one in the black combat gear had dropped to the ground in a hurry.

But just because they'd seen it happen didn't mean they could process what it meant.

"Huh? Sniping?"

"From where?"

"Was that M?"

"No, that was from the opposite direction, right?"

They were as confused as Clarence was, if not more so. Fortunately, whoever was managing the live feed was considerate enough to make it clearer. The angle on the screen switched to a large, clear view of the sniper who had just shot at the two of them.

The player was wearing a gradiated gray-camo poncho and was standing atop the toppled control tower, the tallest altitude around. The sniper had a bolt-action rifle with a boxy body painted in a green-and-brown-camo pattern, with a large scope attached.

Beneath the player's hood, two eyes sparkled—surrounded by brilliant-green hair.

"Oh, it's her! The one who shot Pitohui last time!"

Shirley pulled the bolt with her right hand. It ejected the empty cartridge with tremendous speed and loaded the next one when

she pushed it back forward. From her perfectly upright shooting position, she opened her mouth, canines flashing, to expel the breath from her lungs.

"Die...wild beasts..."

She certainly seemed to be enjoying the game.

"I wonder what Shirley's up to now...?" said a young man in a tree-pattern jacket, standing amid a lengthy stretch of ruined city.

"Dunno. All I know is that she ain't dead so far. Plus, it's not like there's anything we can do to control her now," said another man in the same type of jacket, his hairline receded, from the midst of a forest.

Atop the fallen control tower of the switchyard, the muzzle of Shirley's R93 Tactical 2 swept sideways and came to a crisp stop.

She was firing at a full stand and without any support for her gun. That was the least stable firing position, but the tip of the gun hardly wavered. It merely dipped up and down the slightest bit.

Shirley's pale index finger, which extended bare from a glove that left only that part of her hand exposed, pulled on the trigger.

Holes on the sides of the muzzle emitted brief flames to lower the recoil of the gun firing. The bullet that emerged, wreathed in the heat of the air friction, crossed three hundred yards in a blink—and buried itself into the back of a crouching man.

"Guaaah!"

The man next to the locomotive screamed and toppled forward.

There were three others near him. They'd been hearing the gunshots corresponding to their "teammates" dying on the right for a while, but they never assumed that it was a case of betrayal, just LPFM on the attack, most likely.

So they were caught between rushing over to help or possibly staying in place in case LPFM came into view. All of a sudden, a bullet from out of the blue hit and killed one of them from behind.

He was wearing bulletproof plating on his chest and back. Although the bullet had struck his protective armor, it didn't save his life. The shot left a gaping hole through the armor and his clothes, the glowing damage mark stretching practically from armpit to armpit.

"Huh?"

One of the men turned around, right as the next shot caught him in the chest. He had a new SCAR-H assault rifle, freshly purchased for SJ3, and was on sniping duty but dropped out of the event before he had a chance to fire a single shot with it.

"……"

The third man was unable to process the slaughter around him in time, standing stock-still and making himself a simple target.

The next shot homed in on the center of his body.

"Yikes… There goes another one…"

On the live feed, a huge bullet-hole effect appeared on the stomach of the third victim, who collapsed onto his back. Naturally, he was killed instantly. After the three seconds it took for his hit points to officially hit zero, the DEAD tag appeared over his body.

On another screen, Shirley was exchanging the magazine of her R93 Tactical 2, after she'd fired five shots to kill four players. When she was done, she pushed the bolt forward to load the next bullet. She remained standing atop the fallen control tower during that time.

Her attitude was bold, confident, even heroic. In fact, the poncho flapping behind her in the wind looked like a hero's cape. She had the silhouette of a protagonist.

"Damn, that was rad!"

"I'm assuming she knows there's no enemies around, and that being up high is a major sniping advantage."

"Makes you wish there was some epic BGM playing now."

"Go on! Shoot someone else!"

The crowd was eating it up. Meanwhile, someone who hadn't watched SJ2 wondered, "What's up with that gun…? That's not an antimateriel rifle, is it?"

The effects of the gun were far too powerful to be a normal rifle, with the way that a single shot had spread such wide damage across the chest and stomach, being instantly fatal through bulletproof armor. If its caliber was the size of a large antimateriel rifle, those devastating effects might seem rational, but this gun looked too small for that.

"It's just a typical Blaser R93 Tactical 2. Should be a 7.62 mm, if it's the same one as in SJ2," said one of the audience members who had seen it in action in SJ2. The reason for mentioning the caliber was that the R93 Tactical 2 was a highly adjustable gun with different barrels and ammo magazines.

"That's what I thought. It's too small to be antimateriel. But how does it have such ridiculous power, then?"

The question was met with a period of silence. Eventually, one of the hardest of hardcore gun fanatics in *GGO*, of whom there were many, answered, "This is just a guess, but…"

"And that guess is…?"

"I think that chick's using explosive bullets."

✳   ✳   ✳

Nobody was as pumped up as Shirley was to appear in SJ3.

The woman who had gone into SJ2 thinking "Oh, I don't wanna shoot anyone. I'm all about love and peace for all humankind" was no more. She had died in SJ2.

Now Shirley was a fearsome sniper with bloodlust flowing through her veins. In the video game, that is.

She had trained herself from the ground up in the two-plus months between events. Now she no longer held an ounce of hesitation about shooting anyone within *GGO*. It was "just a game" to her.

In order to get better at it and truly enjoy the game to the fullest, she had spent all her free time outside of work in *GGO*. She'd made her hobby her job, so there was nothing else taking up her attention; and she didn't have a boyfriend, so she had plenty of time.

Shirley hunted monsters in *GGO* and aggressively engaged in PKing when she had the chance, to improve her own personal experience and the stats of her avatar.

Naturally, she wanted to improve her attacking power. She hadn't forgotten the frustration of SJ2. There was no way she could wash that bad taste out of her mouth.

She had taken aim and hit Pitohui right in the head. And yet, that one shot didn't succeed in eliminating all of her health. It hadn't been lethal enough.

But neither did she have any intention of letting go of the R93 Tactical 2. The gun was essentially the same as the normal R93 hunting rifle she had a permit to use in real life (as Mai Kirishima, age twenty-four, resident of Hokkaido, working as a hunter and nature guide), aside from the stock.

The gun was her partner, having gotten her as far as it did in SJ2, and if she was going to appear in SJ3, there was no other gun she could fathom using. It had switchable barrels, so she had the option of going to a larger caliber. She could go from a .308 Winchester (7.62 × 51 mm NATO rounds) to a bigger .300 Winchester Magnum, or a .338 Lapua Magnum.

However, that would give it a different feel from the R93 she fired in real life and throw her off from the instincts she'd built up already. She had a natural feel for "how far this caliber will go before it drops off this much," and that would be lost.

So in the search for a different answer, she arrived at the Bullet Customization skill.

GGO had a number of skills, or special abilities, that players could earn in exchange for experience points, and the Bullet Customization skill was something only people extremely good with their hands could make proper use of.

Shirley ramped up her Dexterity stat as high as she could before she earned the skill. Then she began to fashion more powerful bullets for herself.

As someone who made a living hunting in real life, Shirley naturally knew some things about ammunition. In fact, she knew more than your typical Japanese gun fanatic.

In the military, and within *GGO*, the primary type of ammunition was full metal jacket ammo. That referred to a lead bullet core surrounded in a tougher brass shell—in other words, "jacketed" in "full metal." Often abbreviated to FMJ.

It was easy to recognize them on sight. They were the kind that shone golden, with a pointy end. They had high penetration power, making them ideal for shooting at targets hiding behind cover.

However, the ability to penetrate all the way through a struck target also meant not inflicting all of its potential power on the target as physical damage.

As a contrast to FMJ bullets, there were soft-point, or "jacketed soft-point" bullets, in which just the tip of the bullet was not covered in the stronger metal. These bullets left the softer lead exposed at the end, so even against softer targets, the material would push forward and deform into the organic flesh, expanding like a mushroom head, doing greater damage as it came to a stop.

They were once produced for use in war at a military factory in a place called Dum Dum in British colonial India, giving them the colloquial name of dumdum bullets.

Later, their use was banned in war for the reason of being inhumane and excessive. After that point, it became widely known that dumdum bullets were not to be used in armed conflict.

Then again, there were ways to alter FMJ bullets to inflict more damage on human flesh, and some would argue that humane or inhumane shouldn't be an issue among weapons designed to kill in the first place.

Naturally, both now and in the past, soft-point bullets were used for hunting. When hunting, you needed to kill or immobilize the animal, preferably in one shot. Wild animals with a high tolerance for pain would simply run away if the bullet passed entirely through the body.

They have also been used by police, because they are both damaging to a criminal as well as better at limiting secondary damage that a bullet could still do if it passes through the target and continues onward.

Shirley had begun to work on customizing bullets in search of ever greater power. Her first attempt at soft-point bullets was relatively simple and easy. When she used them against monsters, she could tell that the damage had increased.

But that wasn't enough for her.

"This…isn't going to cut it…"

Her soft-body damage had risen, but the penetrative power against hard objects fell. That meant that if the target was equipped with a bulletproof vest or plate, or was wearing a helmet, the shot would actually be weaker.

She considered switching between FMJ and soft-point bullets according to need, but that would require her to go through the trouble of exchanging magazines.

And more importantly, it introduced a fatal flaw: a slight shift in bullet trajectory when changing between bullets. Different bullets had different weights, and that translated to different trajectories, even if that difference was subtle.

To a one-shot-kill sniper like Shirley, using the same bullet each time and being able to hit the same target each time was extremely important. If this weren't Shirley, but some other random *GGO* player, switching ammo might not be a big deal at all.

The reason for this was, of course, the bullet circle.

It was like an automatic measuring tool for bullet trajectory. It input all relevant variables and calculated where a hypothetical bullet was going to land.

But Shirley (and her companions) did not use a bullet circle. She used her experience, the distance, elevation change, and wind to aim on her own, firing in the same motion that she touched the trigger.

If the bullet circle was a calculator, then Shirley and her fellow hunters were doing mental arithmetic. That also earned them the advantage of never giving their enemies a bullet line to dodge.

"There must be an almighty bullet out there... The perfect something...something...something...," Shirley muttered to herself. Without an answer, she eventually decided, "Guess I'll go kill someone..."

She went off to do some PKing. Maybe if she shot a few people dead, an idea would occur to her. In the game, of course.

On a peaceful weekend afternoon, Shirley hid on the top floor of a building in a ruined city and waited for prey to come along. Being alone and doing nothing for over two hours was very boring, but she'd learned a lot about patience by being a hunter in real life, so it was normal to her.

Then she spotted a group of five players looking satisfied after a hunting session. Luckily, they passed right below her, where she caught them within her scope.

Her aim was vertical—and adjacent to the building. That meant a close range where the bullet would not be very affected by the wind. Gravity wouldn't have a negative effect, either—not when the target was in gravity's path.

As she prepared to shoot each one of them in the head, Shirley spotted something through her zoomed-in scope. Blue plasma grenades, swaying on the back of one of the players.

She fired without hesitation, striking it and causing an explosion. A single bullet succeeded in turning all five of them into blue light together. It must have been quite unpleasant, going from a happy return trip to all of them dead without knowing what had happened.

And to Shirley, the blue explosion was a revelation.

From the window of the dessicated building, she shouted, "That's it! I need to give the bullets explosive power!"

*   *   *

"Explosive bullets...? You can get those?!" mocked one of the audience members in the bar.

"Sure, you can. They're not banned, y'know? What, you think the Geneva convention applies inside of *GGO*?"

"No, I mean, do they actually sell them?"

"They don't—and I don't believe you could conveniently excavate any, so she probably crafted 'em using the Bullet Customization skill. By trial and error."

"You can do that?!"

"I would assume so. You saw what her bullets did to those guys."

"Well… Yeah, I guess so…"

On the TV screen, Shirley went on the move. She slid down the steep angle of the toppled control tower and dropped the last ten feet to the ground when it went vertical. As she landed, she twisted and spun sideways, still holding her gun. It was an excellent redirection of force—otherwise, she might have suffered some fall damage from the jump. It was an agile and natural enough movement that it spoke to the player's natural physical ability.

"Wow. Who is that chick?"

"Don't ask me."

"Wanna try to hit on her later?"

"You always act this way about women… Don't you know that there's no guarantee the real-life player looks like the avatar?"

"So that's why you never get any girls."

"What'd you say?!"

Fortunately for Shirley, she couldn't hear that pointless conversation. Instead, she got back to her feet, held up the R93 Tactical 2 at her waist like a spear, and began to run at full speed.

The gray-camo poncho flapped in the wind as she ran, blending in well with the gravel and concrete around her.

"Is it safe?"

About that moment, Clarence popped her head up to peer around the freight car she was hiding behind, surrounded by four dead bodies. Then she rolled toward the nearest and safest location at the moment—behind the train car's wheels.

Among the dead bodies, she looked at the only one of them she hadn't killed herself—that being her teammate, Sam.

Moments ago, he'd had a huge glowing effect on his chest, but now there was a DEAD tag floating over him, and he was just another body with a peaceful look on his face.

"What kind of bullet was that? It sure packed a punch!" Clarence marveled. She had noticed it, too.

After all, it had inflicted huge damage through thick bulletproof armor that rarely ever allowed bullets to puncture through it. Naturally, she had her own armor in the chest and back of her equipment vest, in a futuristic, sci-fi, ultra-thin style. If she got hit in a vital organ like the lungs or heart, the armor ensured that it at least wouldn't be a one-shot kill.

But somehow, this attack completely nullified that protection.

"Well, I don't know what it is, but…"

Wondering about it wasn't going to give her the answer. So the conclusion was simple.

"Guess I need to keep in mind that a single shot is gonna kill me. Yikes! So scary. War is hell, I tells ya. Good thing this one's just for fun. Whoo-hoo!"

Fortunately, the camera did not capture the sight of Clarence's happy smile as she hid behind the train wheel.

As someone in the bar correctly guessed, Shirley had crafted her own exploding bullets.

In other words, she packed the inside of the bullet with gunpowder and treated it in a way that would make it explode on contact.

In real life, this sort of process would required very high-precision metal-manufacturing machines and industrial processes, but *GGO* was just a game. All you needed was the right material and the command to "produce new bullets," and the character's Dexterity stat would do the rest automatically.

Shirley prepared the most destructive gunpowder she could acquire for her attempt at crafting. After a number of failures, she made it work. It was easier than she expected.

"I did it!" she rejoiced like a child, holding up her own home-made bullet.

The structure of the exploding bullet was not really that complicated. In fact, it was practically primitive.

It started as a pointed-tip FMJ, with the hollowed-out center featuring layers, from top to bottom, of high explosives (very sensitive and powerful gunpowder), then a small primer (the rear cap at the butt of the cartridge that lights up when struck), and lastly, a small striker (a firing pin that hits the primer, one of the most important parts of the gun). That was it.

Once the bullet was released, it would speed toward its target, spiraling rapidly, until the tip made contact. If it met something soft, it would burrow in farther, and if it was bulletproof plating, the nose of the bullet would flatten, spraying the contents out.

In either case, it would cause a massive drop of velocity in the bullet. Inertia would cause the striker inside the bullet to continue pushing forward, like people inside a train hurtling forward when the operator slams on the brakes.

The striker hits the primer, causing a tiny rupture that sets off the explosive, and—*kaboom*. The bullet itself explodes.

The force of the explosion would be limited due to the small amount of gunpowder inside a bullet, but she used the most powerful kind possible in the sci-fi world of *GGO*, so it was more than enough.

The first time Shirley test-shot one of her new bullets, it completely toppled the six-inch-wide tree. When she tried them out on monsters, they proved extremely powerful.

When hitting a living target, the bullet would explode quite deep inside the flesh, delivering plenty of power. Even a huge monster was one and done if she hit its brain.

And when she tried it out on monsters with tough external

armor, as an analogue for human bulletproof armor, she found that it did more damage than she expected. She surmised that this was because the explosion on the surface added significant pressure that transmitted through the organic structure to deliver internal damage.

The bullets' accuracy was perfectly serviceable, so she was able to snipe with as much precision as before.

Against a human target, the exploding bullets would do major damage no matter where they hit. In other words, she didn't have to aim for the insta-kill spots like the brain or spine. She could just aim at the center of the body, the largest, widest part. That way, she could still deliver a fatal shot even if it didn't line up perfectly.

So the explosive bullets seemed like all upside, no downside—except for one very glaring issue.

That would be the price.

Given that one had to buy their own bullets in *GGO*, the cost of daily ammunition was no joke. The reason that guns using well-known standard bullets like 5.56 mm and 7.62 mm NATO rounds were popular was because, pound for pound, those bullets were the cheapest to buy.

The price for Shirley's handmade explosive rounds—given the cost of the raw materials like primer and explosive, the cost of refining and assembling the projectile into a complete bullet, and the frequency of failure—was actually more than fifty times as much as ordinary bullets.

Perhaps a better way to describe that would be to put it in terms of everyday items. "You might like a can of fruit juice, but would you buy one every day if it cost 6,500 yen each time?"

But Shirley did not think twice about it. She used the credits she earned with her period of intense training, and even threw in a little bit of real money as well, until she had amassed two hundred explosive bullets just for SJ3.

If every other team had a full six members, that would make a hundred and seventy-four enemies in total. If she hit each one of them with a single shot, she'd still have spare ammo left over. It wouldn't go that easily, and she'd already missed one shot, but Shirley was having the time of her life as she raced through the switchyard.

"Ha-ha-ha-ha!"

CHAPTER 6

A Woman's Battle

SECT.6

CHAPTER 6
A Woman's Battle

The time was 12:39.

The scan was just about to start, but the five men didn't have time to stop and wait for it.

"What the hell's going on...?"

Just moments before, they'd been split into a pair and a trio, along the left wing of the "crane's wing" formation. They were hiding behind a locomotive and a train car that were still connected on the tracks. Thanks to another vehicle blocking their view, they hadn't actually witnessed Clarence's betrayal or Shirley's sniping.

So when they heard full auto gunfire from the right flank, then a high-pitched sniper's rifle from behind, they had no idea what to make of it.

The five of them gathered up without anyone suggesting they do so and huddled cautiously behind the train engine. One of them posited, "Maybe the guys on the right wing are fighting some new enemy...?"

It wasn't entirely wrong, but another man concluded, "No way, that can't be true! Nobody could've gotten here in time based on the positions of the last scan!" He was right about the scan, so none of the others had a rebuttal to that.

"We're all shooting at LPFM, right? So the gunshots behind us must be some other companions helping out with a sniper rifle, right?" said an optimist.

"Okay, fine. We're not going to learn anything here. Let's move to the right side—but carefully. We want to be able to react to anything that might—"

Ba-koom.

An erupting sound cut him off.

As the others watched, his torso emitted an odd noise, and he toppled sideways. There was a red glow over essentially all of his upper half, as though he'd been flambéed with a blowtorch.

"Sniper!"

The other four promptly scattered. Yet again, they went into a panic, this time about a mysterious source of impossibly powerful bullets. And so they ran, without knowing where or why.

"Tsk!"

But it was Shirley who clicked her tongue in irritation.

She was standing next to a train car with her R93 Tactical 2 in firing position. She'd run across the mazelike switchyard with its many cars and spotted the five unwitting players just five seconds ago. They were six hundred and fifty feet away.

Even with the stiff winds currently blowing, there was no way she'd miss a target as large as a human torso from that range. Shirley's explosive round hit the man in the side as he relayed his plan to the others—and burst inside his flesh. It was an instant kill shot, of course.

She was in good position and wanted to take out at least two of the others, but they split right there on the spot. Two went right, and two went left, promptly hiding behind cars blocking her view.

"Hmph! Then I'll just pick them off starting from the left!"

Shirley spun around, moved behind the train car, and began to run in that direction.

"What the hell? It *was* an enemy! And with a superpowered gun!"

"Just run, dude! Damn, I hate cheap-ass snipers!" whined the two players who had run to the right. They were heading for the right wing of their formation territory. That was the place where all the fierce shooting had been until moments ago, but they preferred to run into battle and find friendly faces than just wander around on their own.

Coming around a container car, they found someone familiar.

"Oh! You two are all right! That's great!"

The player was watching out from a prime spot between two freight cars, situated so he wouldn't be attacked from the front or rear. It was none other than the handsome fellow who showed up late and suggested a plan for them.

What was his name again…?

The audience in the bar saw the whole thing happen.

It was practically an execution.

"No! You better not! He's an enemy!"

The two men approached Clarence and crouched in the shadow of the train car, relieved.

"Go on, get outta there!"

"Behind you! Behind!"

And then Clarence quickly took position just behind them and put a bullet from the AR-57 into the back of their heads.

"Ahhh, well."

"Shit, what was that? An antimateriel rifle?"

"It would have blown up a lot more than that!"

"So what is it, then?!"

"How would I know?!"

The two that ran to the left could only ask questions they didn't have the answer to. They couldn't spare any attention for their surroundings, focusing entirely on running. They sprinted and sprinted, darting from the cover of one car to another.

"Huh?" "Huh?"

And then they saw a certain figure wearing a gray poncho.

*   *   *

The audience watched the men as they ran for their lives. They weren't especially quick characters, but once they got going at full speed, they could dash a significant distance.

The camera focused on them in the center of the frame, making the background speed past. Only those with very good kinetic vision would have noticed the figure in gray entering the frame.

The next moment, it switched to an angle behind Shirley's back, making it clear that the two teams had noticed each other's presence.

"You're close!"

Shirley had been running to get to a good sniping location when she spotted the other two running across her field of view just fifty yards ahead.

"Ah!"

She raised the R93 Tactical 2 to her shoulder without breaking stride.

There was a screaming, high-pitched gunshot.

One of the two runners doubled over, his stomach red, and slid over the gravel, coming to a stop up against the rails. He was dead.

The man running behind him tripped over his friend's corpse—or soon-to-be corpse—and tumbled forward. "Aaaaah!"

He still had all the momentum of running, so despite landing on his face and chest on the rails, he continued to slide. It took him ten feet over onto the next set of tracks.

"Yeow…"

When he looked up in preparation to stand, he saw a figure in a gray poncho rushing at him. Oddly, whoever it was held a long camouflaged stick, as if to stab him like it was a spear.

The tip of it flashed.

"Hya-how! Oh, man!"

"What was that?!"

The audience in the pub roared with delight at Shirley's improvisational technique.

This was called a snapshot—when a shooter instantly took aim and fired at a close enemy. The same term was used in photography, but it had originally come from shooting, referring to the technique of a hunter swiftly and accurately firing at an animal making an abrupt, unexpected appearance.

It was a style of shooting that every player in *GGO* had experienced before, of course, but it took major skill to pull it off with a sniper rifle. And beyond that...

"That was a running snapshot..."

"Insane."

Shirley had done it while on the run. She'd aimed with her rifle and fired while at a full sprint.

From spotting them to shooting had taken less than a second. That shot had hit the stomach of the first man just like any other shot she might take.

The exploding bullet was worth every bit of its fifty-times cost. If it had been a normal bullet, it would have penetrated through the stomach and certainly not delivered a fatal amount of damage on its own.

And because it was an instant kill and caused the man to fall, it had the added benefit of tripping up the second one. That man wasn't in any state to fight back yet, so she could have stopped and taken careful aim, but Shirley did not slow down. She couldn't rule out the presence of other foes around.

She used the R93 Tactical 2's extremely fast loading mechanism to fire again, killing the second man—while still on a run, of course. She was like an archer on horseback in the olden days.

Shirley kept her eyes open for other threats and, finding nothing for the moment, finally came to a stop and took cover behind a train car. She still had two shots left but switched out the magazine anyway.

"Good thinking, lady."

"Man, she's good. She can snipe; she can snapshot..."

On the bottom of the screen, the number five glowed.

"That means the allied team is wiped out," said another audience member. He glanced over at the adjacent table, where the man in the beret was seated alone, practically crying with frustration.

"......"

It was ten seconds after 12:41.

The fourth Satellite Scan was over.

"Damn, didn't have time to take a look!" lamented Clarence as she hovered over the bodies of the two men she'd just executed.

The fourth scan had passed in less than a minute, and her device did not display any team dots. A map would pop up, but it wouldn't even tell Clarence her own current location. That was the kind of unhelpfulness players could look forward to in Squad Jam.

"Ah-whuh?"

Clarence suddenly leaped back in surprise at the water that appeared under her feet without a sound. The sea was upon her.

It spread in a line across the ground, moving at about the speed of a brisk walking pace, steadily growing higher as it filled the switchyard without abiding.

Like lines of sandbags, the sets of rails briefly slowed the advance of the water, but being rails, they weren't very tall. More water would push up from behind until it soon rushed over the metal tracks. If anything, the speed of the ocean's progress seemed to be picking up.

"Uh-oh, this looks bad!" Clarence yelped, boots kicking up water as she ran.

After she left, the two dead bodies remaining silently sank beneath the rising water.

"Oh, look how far it's come..."

Shirley was noticing the approaching water, too. Looking out from the freight car she was taking cover behind, she saw the scenery about three hundred yards ahead was being replaced by water.

The flat ground was covered with water the same dull, leaden gray as the sky above, turning the cars and engines into little islands—islands that promised nothing but slow, peaceful death if you got stuck on one.

Fighting against a powerful foe and getting shot to death was one thing, but Shirley was not about to let herself get knocked out of SJ3 from drowning.

Like Clarence, she wasn't in a position to check the scan as it was happening, so she gave up on the idea of pursuing combat for the next ten minutes.

"Oh well. Guess I'll withdraw from this battlefield for now…"

But deep down, she still wanted to fight.

Shirley knew that nobody was going to be able to check the locations on the scan and know where she was. It was thanks to her plan.

It was in the waiting area of SJ3, meaning just before the start of the event, that Shirley relayed her idea to her four teammates. The men could hardly be blamed for their incredulity. After all, she told them, "I'll be acting alone as soon as we start. I want the rest of you to split up and just run free across the map. I have myself designated as the last member to become leader."

"Huh? What?" Some of her teammates had no idea what she meant.

"Oh, I get it… So that's your plan…" While others got the gist of it at once.

"Wh-what do you mean?"

"Only the leader shows up during the scan, you know? If all five of us run around separately, then even if they track down our dot to finish us off, they can only find and kill one of us every ten minutes."

"Oh, now I see…"

"Then the next member becomes the leader, so even if the team leader gets killed within every ten-minute span…"

"Then they won't know Shirley's location for at least forty minutes! But won't acting alone be dangerous…?" said one of the teammates, before stopping himself.

Setting themselves aside, Shirley had put in a lot of work to better her character, and she was probably more likely to survive on her own than they were. Given their relative lack of experience, they might actually just hold her back.

In a rush, she explained, "I'm going to look for as many one-hit kills as I can get with my exploding rounds. I've got a number of different camo ponchos for different environments. If I think they're too tough, I'll lay low and stay quiet. You'll all find it easier to flee when alone, and you're good enough to shoot without a bullet line if you have a clear shot. Maybe I'm being overly optimistic, but I don't think you'll go down that quickly."

Then she paused and added, "Plus, remember the plan the beret guy pitched to us, to gather when we see the signal flare go up? We can use that. If they get a big team together, all those people are going to be occupied with their fight for the first thirty or forty minutes. We'll be able to hit them from behind or get the chance to slip away."

"All right, that makes sense now…and I can't think of a better plan. Anyone else?"

There was no argument from the others.

Shirley's team had started SJ3 in the town that took up the northern part of the map, almost smack in the middle between east and west, but at the very northern edge, right along the water. The approaching ocean became very clear to them, right away.

"Best of luck, everyone. If all goes well, we'll have a drink afterward. I'm turning off the comm now," Shirley said. She donned a gray-camo poncho, called A-TACS AU from her inventory, then rushed off with her R93 Tactical 2 in hand. She was gone, around the side of a building in no time.

"Well, guess we'll see how far we get…"

"Uh-huh!"

"Got it!"

"We're like civilian troops protecting Hokkaido from invasion!"

The four men exchanged fist bumps, hoisted their hunting rifles, and went their separate ways. Unlike Shirley, they had kept their comms open, so they could talk if they felt like it.

And now, forty minutes later, none of Shirley's teammates had died yet. The widespread plan to team up had worked out in their favor. Many of the teams in the game were preoccupied with taking out one of the top squads and had paid no attention to KKHC.

So all four of her comrades were currently alive and well in various locations.

Of course, it was only because they didn't want to attack anyone else and get people angry at them, so they were engaging in the saddest option of all: running and hiding and trying not to be noticed.

Shirley decided to relocate for now. She checked her teammates' HP up in the left corner of her view. It seemed like a miracle that all of them were completely unharmed.

"Thanks, guys. That gives me more of a chance to kick ass," she muttered, prioritizing her own enjoyment over the safety of her teammates.

Between the results of the scan and the red signal flare, it was very clear to her that LPFM were on the other side of the switchyard. That team included Pitohui, whom Shirley had failed to take out in SJ2, and Llenn, who had been the one to knock her target out instead. She burned with desire to finish them off herself this time, but she decided that the circumstances weren't ideal for a sneak attack.

They obviously weren't going to merely sink into the water; they would be surviving through some means or another. And as long as they were alive, she would have another chance to come across them.

For now, she was going to retreat to the interior of the island to get away from the water, and she could wait for that chance to arrive from there.

When Shirley started to run, it took no more than thirty seconds for her to cross paths with Clarence, who was also going at full speed.

"What's this?"

Clarence wasn't expecting to see the sniper at such close range. She just assumed the gunshots earlier were from the other men in the alliance. Besides, a sniper rushing in was no longer acting like a sniper. It didn't make sense.

"Huh?"

For her part, Shirley didn't expect to see an enemy rushing *toward* the direction of a gunshot.

Clarence leaped out from behind the overturned engine as Shirley emerged from the side of the tanker car.

Unluckily for Shirley, Clarence's cover was a toppled locomotive. If it had been a car resting on the tracks, the sniper would have been able to see the other side between the wheels and spot the approaching pair of feet.

Unfortunately for Clarence—well, it was simply bad luck that she'd been running that way at all.

The two spotted each other at the ultra-short distance of about twenty yards.

"Hya!" Clarence shrieked.

"Ah!" Shirley gasped. They pointed their weapons at each other from the waist position.

Clarence's reaction wasn't slow, by any means, but Shirley had alrcady pulled off two successful snapshots, and she won out here, too.

The R93 Tactical 2 let out a high-pitched blast before the AR-57 could. Her special exploding round roared and smashed into its target.

"Gyahk!"

Right into the body of the AR-57 in Clarence's hand.

It was powerful enough to reduce the gun to just one step short of utterly scrapped. It was out of SJ3 and wouldn't be usable again until she took it to a gun shop for repairs.

They came to a stop ten yards apart right at the moment that the deflected AR-57 fell onto the rails.

Shirley pulled the bolt, expelling the empty, pushed the bolt back, loading the next bullet—but not before Clarence's arm darted.

She grabbed the grip of the Five-Seven pistol in her right holster. With blazing speed, she pulled it loose as Shirley finished reloading and cackled happily while unloading a series of shots.

"Hya-haaa!"

"Urgh!"

Shirley fired as a bullet hit her left shoulder. The shift in her balance caused the shot to go wide, only grazing Clarence's shoulder by a fraction of an inch and sending up sparks from the metal exterior of the train engine just behind her.

Clarence's second shot passed over Shirley's head and pierced her hood as it went. It revealed Shirley's green hair, the camo cap she wore backward, and the trio of black lines she'd drawn on her face.

The markings on her face were made with mud the last time. Now she'd replaced them with black camouflage cosmetics. The way the pattern ran across her pale skin made it look like some fierce animal pelt.

"Wha—? Eh?"

Clarence's third and fourth shots were not followed by another.

The bullets hit Shirley's arm and side, but they mostly deflected off and into the distance. The two faced each other, guns silent, from just thirty feet apart.

"Well, well! You're a woman, too! Hey, no moving now!" Clarence said brightly, keeping her gun trained on Shirley with one hand. Her handsome features were turned upward into a dazzling smile.

Shirley paused with her open hand against the bolt handle.

"Too...? So you're a woman?"

Without moving her aim, Clarence replied jauntily in English, *"Yes, I do."*

"Uh, I think you mean *Yes, I am.* Do you...actually know English?"

"Sorry. And now..."

The crowd in the bar witnessed their sudden meeting and the furious firefight that immediately broke out. Then they paused and seemed to be talking about something.

Unless the camera was very close and the people were shouting, the Squad Jam live feed did not pick up voices.

"Wonder what they're saying..."

"C'mon, guys, pick up the voices for us!" the audience complained.

In fact, the content of their conversation was not really worth listening to.

"Then prepare to eat lead. Or in English...*die!*"

Clarence opened fire at the same moment Shirley jumped sideways.

"Ha!"

She took a huge sidestep to the left, in the direction of Clarence's dominant hand, which was said to be harder for a shooter to follow. This helped her evade the bullet lines and the shots that followed them, while she loaded her next shot with the bolt so fast that it left an afterimage.

The muzzle of the R93 Tactical 2 stopped perfectly over Clarence's target.

"Wh-what?" Clarence was shocked. How did she dodge pistol shots at this distance? But there was no stopping the firing now.

There was the much louder and deeper report of a rifle, which would never be confused for pistol shots. The exploding round hit Clarence and blew up—on her right knee.

"Shit!" Shirley swore.

She saw it happen. The instant she pulled the trigger, one of Clarence's 5.7 mm bullets hit the body of the R93 Tactical 2, knocking her aim off course. If not for that, her shot would have hit Clarence square in the middle of the stomach. Whether it was a fluke or had been aimed that way on purpose, it kept Shirley from scoring the instant kill.

Of course, the exploding round ensured that her leg did not remain in any form. Clarence's entire lower leg turned red and split off from the knee. Without its support, she toppled over to the right.

"Gya-ha-ha!"

Even through all this, Clarence cackled and fired her gun. The Five-Seven had a twenty-round magazine, which was a lot for a pistol. Its exterior was entirely made of plastic and looked like a toy. It fired easily and brightly, as though channeling its owner's delight.

"Gahk! Gahk!"

The bullets struck Shirley all over, including on her special gun.

Flop. Clarence toppled onto her right elbow.

Thump. Shirley dropped to her knees at the same moment.

They were about twenty feet apart.

The two froze, separated by five sets of rails.

Clarence went onto her side on the gravel. Her Five-Seven's slide was retracted, indicating the chamber was absent of bullets. She had about 40 percent of her hit points left.

Shirley was down on her right knee atop the rail tie, propping herself up with the R93 Tactical 2. Bright little bullet-hole effects glowed all over. The damage was especially bad to her legs—each one had three shots in it. She would be feeling a lot of numbness.

Her HP bar was just over 20 percent, way down in the red zone.

"You've really done it now...," Shirley growled, loathing in her voice.

"That's my line! You just blasted my leg right off, you jerk!" Clarence said angrily, though she was still smiling. "But I've got the advantage! I need to replace my magazine. But you shouldn't fire that gun at all. You know why, I assume?"

"...Son of a...bitch," Shirley swore, in poor sportsmanship. She was furious, but her opponent was right. There was a large, deep gash in the top of the barrel from where the bullet had struck it—a bold, lifesaving shot as her opponent fell to the ground.

If the damage from the bullet got inside her gun, meaning that any point of the perfectly cylindrical barrel was punched inward, any shot she fired would stop there. And when a bullet stopped, the combustion pressure of the gunpowder behind it would build up to incredible levels until the barrel ruptured. And Shirley was shooting exploding bullets. It could blow up the weapon right in her face.

In a worst-case scenario, it might ruin her precious gun forever.

In Squad Jam, where there were no weapon or item drops, that would leave her without a means of replacing it. The only way would be to buy a new one.

And to add insult to injury, the blast might damage her enough to knock her out of SJ3 altogether, at the same time that it destroyed her gun. Just in case, she could switch her ammo to normal bullets and hold the gun up over her head to give it a test-fire that might tell her if it was still battle-worthy.

But the one-legged woman across from her knew that, too, and she wasn't going to give her the chance to try it out.

"You're not going anywhere. I watched the video of SJ2 very closely. Your team was real fixated on their rifles, and none of you had pistols. So I know that I have all the time in the world to change my magazine and shoot you. Easy peasy," she said, certain of her victory.

Clarence's left hand moved toward the pouch at her side where she kept the Five-Seven's extra magazines.

"Hey," Shirley called out, still crouched. "Do you know how a hunter performs a finish on an animal that's been immobilized?"

Clarence's head inclined questioningly. Her free hand grabbed the backup magazine. "Did you say 'fish'? Like...sashimi?"

"Finish. As in, to finish off."

"I don't know, how do you? Tell a funny joke and make them die laughing?"

"Wrong!"

Shirley let go of the R93 Tactical 2. She straightened up her body, still glowing with painful-looking bullet effects, and began to rush at Clarence.

"What's that?"

Clarence pulled out the magazine with her left hand and disengaged the empty magazine from the Five-Seven with her right. Then she lifted her hands together to combine the two, slamming the magazine into the handle and pulling the slide stop to load the first bullet. It was a quick, efficient motion that spoke to her familiarity with the pistol.

Lastly, she pointed it right at Shirley.

"Huh?"

Shirley was nowhere to be seen on the ground.

"Shaaa!"

Clarence heard the hissing cry from up above. A human body plunged onto her from the sky.

"Gagehk!"

Shirley's knee plunged into Clarence's stomach. She had jumped high before Clarence could shoot her and used gravity to drive her knee downward. Her left hand reached out to grab

Clarence's right arm and hold it down before it could point the Five-Seven at her.

"Oh no you don't!"

Earlier, they'd been shooting, and now they were grappling, one woman with her knees stuck onto the other with one arm pinned.

Then Shirley said "You do *this*!" and demonstrated the answer to the question of how a hunter properly finishes an immobilized animal.

First, she used her free hand to reach across her body under the poncho for her final weapon: the hilt of a large knife, similar in profile to a katana, about a foot in length.

This knife, known as a ken-nata, came in handy for just about anything when a hunter ventured into the mountains. It could be used to cut branches out of the way or chop wood for kindling.

And a single thrust to the heart, given its length, could finish off an animal without any needless suffering. Out of habit from hunting, Shirley and the other KKHC members kept one on their belts at all times.

She'd never used it in *GGO*. It was more like a good luck charm, a fashion item that identified their way of life.

Until now.

"Gyaargh!"

A dull, gurgling shout escaped Clarence's throat. Shirley's ken-nata was jammed eight inches into her left flank, right on the side where the armor plating of her vest offered no protection.

"Oh! Sorry, I missed the heart," Shirley said, knee on Clarence's stomach and hunting knife in her side. "I'll put you at ease right now."

The green-haired woman leaned in, a gentle look on her face. She wouldn't forget the proper respect for her prey.

"I could go for a kiss before that..." Clarence grimaced against the virtual pain up and down her side. She could see her hit-point readout dropping slowly, from green to yellow.

But that was about it, because it was just her flank. If it had been her heart like Shirley intended, she would've been down to zero by now.

"No thanks!" snapped Shirley, yanking her arm upward, knife and all.

"Gaaah!"

The tip of the blade, now even deeper in Clarence's body, turned and approached her heart. She felt the ugly—even when virtual—sensation of a foreign object plunging inside her body. The speed of her HP loss rose.

"Gaaaahh... Screw youuuu...!"

Clarence reached the one part of her body she could move, her left arm, behind her waist. She opened the pouch there and took out what was inside.

Her hit points were in the red zone. Not much time left.

But enough.

Clarence's left hand came up to her face, and she put what she was holding in between her gleaming teeth.

"Huh?"

Shirley saw a dully shining object. It looked like a small pineapple—sized to fit into the palm—but a metallic gun gray, with a large lever attached. She didn't need to have used one before to recognize a hand grenade.

With a crisp snap, Clarence popped the lever off, then pulled out the safety pin with her teeth. "This is for you," she said with a smile, right before her hit points dropped to zero, and she died.

The strength went out of her right arm, which had been trying to shoot Shirley, and her other arm dropped to the ground as well.

Even after death, Clarence did not let go of the grenade.

Shirley saw the DEAD sign pop into existence over the head of the person she was holding down.

Then her vision went white with an explosion.

This is one prize I won't be eating, she thought as the storm of expanding heat, air, and shrapnel consumed her.

*   *   *

All of this—from the furious close-range firefight, to the loss of limbs, to the leaping stab, to the self-destruction as the first one died—was clearly visible to the audience at the bar.

It had been a close-up fight, so the camera zoomed in nice and close. It caught Shirley's ken-nata stabbing into her opponent, the change in their expressions, and the blast of polygons as they both exploded from the grenade, all at dynamic, detailed angles.

"Eugh…"

"Nasty…"

"Brutal."

"You'd think they would show some discretion," admitted the hardened virtual soldiers.

When the two women vanished from SJ3, the men of KKHC noticed immediately.

"Oh! Shirley died!"

It was clear because they could see their teammate's hit points dropping rapidly on the left edge of their vision, until they ran out entirely a few dozen seconds later.

"Aww, so much for that…"

"Dammit!"

They were having a remote conversation from various points across the map, where each member was hiding individually.

"Oh! Whoa! Crap, I got spotted! I gotta run—"

The leader's voice abruptly cut out. His hit points dropped incredibly fast, straight down to zero, and the leader mark dropped to the next man on the list.

It was clear that the last scan had revealed his location to a powerful nearby team that bore down on his location and picked him off. Once he was within their sights, a lone hunter with limited personal power didn't stand a chance. That left three members of KKHC alive.

"Yep, that's it."

"This is as far as we get."

"Better than I thought, actually," the three of them agreed, before proceeding to their next course of action.

The trio voluntarily chose to leave SJ3.

*   *   *

12:47.

Shirley's and Clarence's silent bodies were sinking under the surface of the water. The grenade blast had utterly destroyed their upper halves, but since Squad Jam bodies were left in pristine condition, the dispersed polygons silently coalesced into their original shape, like some kind of resurrection magic.

At this moment, the two of them were counting out the ten minutes in the waiting area, perhaps regretting the mistakes they made or complimenting themselves on a job well done.

Or maybe they had already logged out and gone back to the real world.

"Ah, here's two more…"

Llenn glanced at the two bodies submerged in water. Enemies or not, virtual world or not, it wasn't exactly pleasant to see human corpses. There was a note of sadness in her voice.

"Let's see? Ooooh, mutual takedown. May you rest in peace," Pitohui added. She made a praying motion.

"Isn't that the player who gave Llenn the ammo last time? I think it is," said Fukaziroh. It was a sharp observation.

"The other one's the girl who sniped Pito. I'm certain of that," M noted. He was definitely attentive.

LPFM was making very slow progress through the switchyard—on a truck. It was a small brown military truck, with a roof over the bed and the sides of the cab covered with armor plating that had clearly been custom attached.

Those who watched the broadcast of SJ1 might remember the

truck that SHINC used at the end to cross a vast distance very quickly. This was the exact same data—er, model of vehicle.

M was driving, of course, while the other three had their faces and guns poking just a little bit out of the armor siding of the truck bed. They were ready to shoot if the need arose.

While it was small for its type, the military truck had large tires and a high ground clearance. Over half of the tires were currently underwater, but the engine intake and exhaust were higher, giving them room to spare to keep running. M had the truck running slowly and carefully, at almost the same speed as the advance of the sea.

The two bodies steadily vanished behind them. Llenn watched them go, until the only things visible were the DEAD signs hanging over the surface of the water, and wondered, "Did they fight here and kill everyone else...?"

Pitohui replied, "I bet so!" Then, in a bubbly tone of voice that baffled Llenn, she continued, "Gosh, they were pretty impressive! I like them! I like them a lot!"

Nothing good comes from being liked by Pito, Llenn thought but wisely did not say.

M's plan for them might as well have been literally called the Backs to the Water plan.

They didn't leave the black freight car until the ocean was almost upon them, and they moved forward with the water.

When she first heard the plan, Llenn was annoyed. Why did they have to put extra pressure on themselves like this? But when she heard his two reasons, they did make sense to her.

For one, the enemies surrounding them had to deal with the fear of the encroaching sea, and few of them were likely to be bold enough to stand their ground knowing that it was coming for them.

For the other, LPFM had the truck. It was located atop an auto-rack car for transporting automobiles by rail, and M knew that they could use it. He'd had the time to inspect and confirm this—while Llenn had been running around drawing attention.

The idea was to hole up inside the freight car and thin out the enemy numbers, then wipe out the remainder when they got jumpy or use the truck to blaze through the encirclement if needed...

"And in the end, we didn't need to do anything..."

Llenn was stunned.

After Pitohui had used her lightsword to cut a big hole in the side of the black freight car so they could leave, they heard gunshots. In fact, it sounded like the enemy was shooting at each other. M picked up on that and suggested a change in plans.

They decided to adopt a strategy of doing nothing. They filed into the truck and lay low for a little while.

The sounds of battle got fiercer as they went along, until distant sniping was added to the mix. It became a tremendous, chaotic clatter.

"Geez, it sounds like people are dying out there..."

"Well, uh, *yeah*, Fuka."

"Why can't people learn to stop fighting? If we could all just speak from the heart over a beer or two, the world could see eye to eye and find peace."

"Pito, I just want to ask you, because I can't tell for sure, but you are joking, right?" Llenn snapped. In the meantime, the sound was getting even louder. Finally, there was what sounded like a grenade blast, and then it was suddenly silent.

Without any audible combat nearby, and the sea filling in under their position, they started up the truck. When they approached, slowly and cautiously, they found only the dead bodies of their foes ahead. There was no one alive to demand they emerge with their hands up.

Llenn was very curious about how exactly the last two had simultaneously knocked each other out, but there was no answer to that question here.

"Don't worry about it! Just be thankful we got it easier! The battle's heading into the middle section now," Fukaziroh said optimistically.

"I guess you're right," Llenn admitted.

It was a stroke of luck that they didn't need to use up any of their ammo to get out of their trapped position. And the battle wasn't over yet. In fact, they hadn't even started fighting with SHINC, which was her entire reason for being here.

They'd had the time to watch the fourth scan happen earlier, which confirmed that both SHINC and MMTM were still alive. As were the Machine-Gun Lovers. The number of teams remaining at the time was still in double digits. But the nearby shooting had reduced the number while the scan was still ongoing.

They heard the last throes of battle and the grenade explosion just after the scan was over, so it seemed like they were getting very close to the final "six to eight teams" requirement for the special rule to come into play.

Of course, they didn't know where and how that would happen. Llenn asked, "What do you think? Are we under eight teams by now?"

"Maybe, but maybe not yet. Maybe baguette. With vinaigrette," said Fukaziroh, who didn't seem very concerned. "What it all comes down to is: We're fighters. Whatever happens, we fight to the death, la-da-dee, la-da-doo."

"What was that at the end?"

"I dunno, like the sound of warriors wandering across the wasteland. With the wind and stuff. You know?"

"I don't know—and that's all I know."

Llenn decided that she was just going to wait for the fifth scan.

CHAPTER 7

SECT.7

Special Rule Takes Effect

CHAPTER 7
Special Rule Takes Effect

12:49 PM.

The truck carrying Llenn's team made its way out of the switch-yard at last, unharassed by any enemies. Most of the switchyard itself was now underwater.

The border between the yard and its adjacent territory was a rusty fence. Two fences, in fact, meant to keep people out of the area, but M drove the truck right over the flimsy chain-link barriers.

Ahead of them was grassland.

Naturally, it was very easy to get the lay of the land once they were there. No manmade structures blocked any of the view. There were many rolling bulges and divots in the ground with room to hide a person. The land gently rose as it approached the center of the island.

A variety of grasses covered about 80 percent of the plain, all of them a rotten-green color. They looked like they would be fatal in the span of a single night if ingested.

The grass was about a foot or two tall, enough to hide a person lying down, but which wouldn't offer protection against any bullets, of course. As usual, the visual range was poor, so it was still impossible to tell what lay atop the tallest hill, in the UNKNOWN area.

M commanded, "Everyone get ready to disembark. Watch the perimeter after that."

"Come on, M, drop us off at the house on top of the hill. You really want to force all these girls to walk?" Fukaziroh complained.

"We're almost out of gas."

"You can move it with spirit, right? That's a thing, isn't it?"

"I didn't bring any with me today."

"Guess we'll just have to spin the pedals, then. They put those on all trucks, don't they?"

"This one must be defective."

"Damn. Gotta complain to the event hosts after this is over."

"All set…and out!"

They jumped out of the rear of the truck bed while it was still moving. This little stunt wasn't for showing off flashy action, but to make it harder to get shot. Filing out of the vehicle after stopping it just meant that you were offering a stationary target, so it was better to hop out while it was still moving, even if slow.

The three women hopped out and went low, making themselves small targets, and found dips in the ground a good distance apart to hide. Lastly, M stopped the truck about fifty yards away, tossed his backpack out first, then leaped out of the driver's seat and got flat on the ground.

With each of them watching out in one of the cardinal directions, they prepared for the fifth scan to start. Once again, only M would be checking the map.

12:50 arrived without a sound.

Llenn peered out cautiously through blades of grass. In her ear, M reported, "Seven surviving teams. Not one within fifteen hundred. You can all look at the scan."

"Fifteen hundred," of course, was about the distance (in meters) at which one needed to worry about long-distance sniping. That was about a mile. It was the effective range of a .50-caliber sniper rifle or SHINC's anti-tank rifle. In other words, the range that you could effectively aim and deliver damage with the power of the bullet.

With the wind strong today, it was very unlikely that a single shot at that distance would hit the target, but even a lucky hit could be fatal, so there was nothing wrong with being cautious.

"All right! Time to check this out!" Fukaziroh crowed. Llenn sat down on the ground and pulled out her Satellite Scan terminal.

When she brought up the map on the screen, she yelped, "Yipes! Look how small it is now!"

The shape of the island was still a square, but what had started at a bit over six miles to a side was now no more than two and a half. The switchyard in the southwest, town in the northern corners, forest to the east, and rocks in the southeast were all underwater now.

And as usual, the UNKNOWN label sat in the middle.

The scan moved slowly, so Llenn had plenty of time to count the dots and tap them to bring up the team names. They, of course, were the dot in the southwest part of the map. As M said, there was no one within a mile of them. Of course, any of the teams could be using a decoy strategy, leaving the leader behind so the rest of the team could roam undetected.

She touched the dot in the southeast corner. "Please...yes!"

It was SHINC. They were still alive. They were around two miles away—and there were no teams in between.

Just about two and a half miles north of SHINC, in the northeast corner, was MMTM. Their rival was still alive and well.

On the north end of the map was none other than ZEMAL. Back in SJ1, they were just a rabble of machine-gun-loving weirdos, but they had grown much tougher since then.

The remaining three were in the northwest corner, the upper left part of the map. Two of the dots glowed about two-thirds of a mile apart. They could even be in battle at the moment.

She tapped the one on the right, which brought up the name TOMS. That was unfamiliar to her. They appeared to be new to Squad Jam.

The one on the left was DDL, which Llenn did remember. They'd been in SJ1, but not SJ2. She couldn't remember much

THE 3rd SQUAD JAM
FIELD MAP

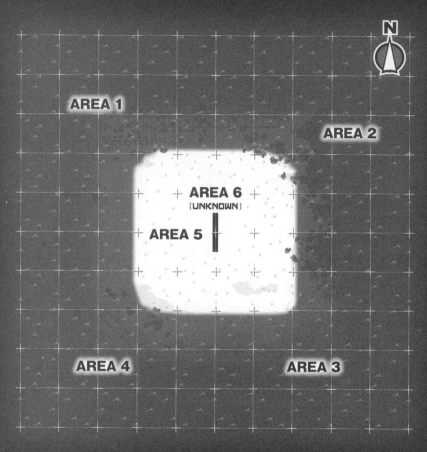

AREA 1 : City

AREA 2 : Forest

AREA 3 : Wasteland

AREA 4 : Switchyard

AREA 5 : Hill

AREA 6 : Unknown

about their preferred gear, but she did recall from watching the tape that they had fallen prey to SHINC in the desert.

The last one was in the middle of the water in the upper-left corner, in the part of the map that had formerly been the city. In other words, they'd been left on top of one of the tall buildings there.

Llenn remembered being surprised at that earlier, too, so she took the time to tap the dot, which revealed the name T-S.

Aha. So it's you. I see.

She had conflicting feelings about that. She'd never forget the name T-S. That was the team of six dressed up in future sci-fi soldier armor with their faces hidden.

The last time around, they rode atop the fortress walls on bicycles, until at the very end, when Llenn and Fuka were exhausted from fighting Pitohui, they picked the girls off from a long distance.

She wasn't going to hold a grudge—competition was competition. In fact, she was even a bit grateful that they'd waited until she had already finished off Pitohui.

"The people stuck out on the ocean can't move from there, right?" Fukaziroh wondered. That was probably correct.

"Those were the champions from last time! What are they doing?!" Pitohui demanded, incensed. But she wasn't scolding them for incompetence; she was frustrated that she wouldn't have the chance to kill them herself.

Llenn understood exactly how she felt but chose not to say anything.

*   *   *

Meanwhile, the members of T-S were sadly fading into the distance atop their building.

"Who was it? Who said that if we took up a high position, we'd be able to shoot off any oncomers?!"

"That was me! But nobody argued against it!"

"Stop it, you two. This is embarrassing."

"Man, I'm so bored…"

"I haven't taken a single shot so far."

"Neither have I! Dammit…"

The soldiers in full armor sat with their arms around their knees, like action figures arranged in poses. The GR9 machine gun arranged on a bipod looked like a life-size toy next to them.

They had begun SJ3 in the northwest corner, in the middle of the city. As the defending champions, they came into SJ3 with high spirits, but in the pub just before the event started, they learned of a dramatic turn of events.

Yes, by being invited into the proposed alliance of teams, they learned that they, too, were targets. The color of their signal flares, incidentally, was purple.

"That's messed up! It's bullying!"

"No way! We're gonna get surrounded right away!"

It was easy to imagine enemy squads converging on their position as soon as the first scan started. Visibility was poor in the city, so even if they tried to escape, it was quite possible that they'd get trapped on multiple sides.

The only area in which they truly excelled was in defense, thanks to their full-body protective armor. If they got into a firefight with multiple enemies, they didn't stand a chance—and they knew it.

"We've gotta focus on defense!"

"Yeah, let's find advantageous terrain and set up a defensive perimeter."

So they decided upon an ambush plan. Coincidentally, there was a tall building right in front of their starting position. Probably twenty stories? It looked like a luxury high-rise apartment next to the beach.

One of the members of the squad suggested they take a position at the very top of that sturdy-looking building, where they could fire down on anyone who attempted to come after them.

A team in SJ1 had occupied a spot inside of the crashed spaceship.

Coincidentally, it was similar to the way they raced around atop the castle walls last time to avoid danger. So they couldn't be blamed for feeling like this strategy might work, too.

"Let's go!"

"All right! Hurry!"

They'd moved right away for the seaside high-rise, rather than waiting for the 12:10 scan first. The interior was desolate. Naturally, the elevators didn't work anymore, so they used the one emergency stairwell to move upward.

On the way, they pulled some furniture out of rooms to place on the stairs, and even laid a few traps with hand grenades. If any of the enemy teams tried to go into the building to chase after them, they'd get a nasty surprise.

It was quite a trek to get up all twenty-five floors, but within ten minutes, they had gotten it done and emerged on the roof.

"Huh?"

And when the first scan came in, they came to understand the terrible reality around them.

The building they were standing on top of was now in the midst of the rising waters.

After the first scan ten minutes into the game, a purple signal flare went up, and six other teams came flocking into the city. All twenty-four of the members were fired up and ready to take down the defending champions of Squad Jam, but when they saw the ocean before them and the very tall building sprouting up about two hundreds yards out into the water, in which the enemy was hiding, they came to a simple conclusion.

"This is impossible…"

But vehicles were common in Squad Jam. They searched the area, assuming there would certainly be a boat somewhere, but found nothing. The height of the water was up over a person's head, meaning that there was no longer any way to get to the building.

There was a brief bit of gun combat between the ground and the roof of the building in the meantime, but the distance was so great, and the combatants so well-covered, that both sides quickly realized it was a waste of bullets.

Eventually, one team decided to break away and go after Team LPFM in the southwest switchyard. Another team joined the fight against the powerhouse MMTM in the east.

At last, after 12:20, the four remaining teams made their decision.

"Change of plans! We're gonna kill you guys here! Let's have an urban battle!"

"Sounds fun! Let's do this! You're on, bitches!"

"I'm in, too! I don't wanna bother with traveling long distances! But if we fight right now, we're just wasting our lives, right?"

"Let's count to a hundred! No, make it two hundred, and then we fight!"

They were going to make the most of SJ3, like kids looking forward to a game of tag.

The resulting battle was quite a lot of fun for the audience watching in the bar.

"Do you think we can shoot those guys duking it out from up here?"

"Nah, it's way too far away."

"This is so boring."

But the members of T-S didn't get much more out of it than the sound of distant gunfire.

And so, time passed mercilessly for T-S, without them having any say in the matter. A stalemate appeared to fall over the city, as they stopped hearing just about any kind of gunfire, until it started up again in the midst of the fifth Satellite Scan.

It was a quick rattling report in the distance. The shooting stopped very soon, right as they noticed a change in the scan.

"Hey! One of the teams vanished!"

"You're right. That's the end of DDL."

One of the white dots on the city end of the map turned gray. That was most likely the work of TOMS, the dot adjacent to it. They would have seen on the scan that they were very close, indeed, and promptly started fighting. It happened all the time in Squad Jam.

That left just six teams in SJ3.

"Uh-oh, there goes one! Man, can't people just calm down and take it easy during the scan?" chattered Fukaziroh, who was watching the map in the middle of the grassy plain.

"That's sure to kickstart this special rule, then. I wonder what it is," said Pitohui through the comm.

I mean, who really cares? Llenn silently retorted.

As long as she could fight with SHINC, she didn't mind what the rules were. And given their present locations, they were definitely going to fight SHINC next—or perhaps the team after that. It was time to buckle down!

This was the perfect situation for Llenn. She was very happy at the moment. She just knew that it was all a very personal desire of hers, so she kept quiet about it.

12:52 PM.

After a very long and slow scan, the six remaining dots vanished from the map.

Breeep!

The Satellite Scan terminals emitted a totally new sound. A very obnoxious and grating buzzer sound.

"Whoa! Geez, that startled me! Knock it off, that's bad for my heart!" Fukaziroh snapped, furious.

Llenn was startled, too, and she quickly pulled the device back out of her shirt pocket. Despite the switch being turned off, the screen was glowing. There was a message on it:

"In thirty seconds, the special rule will be announced on this screen and go into immediate effect."

*   *   *

"Oh! Here it comes! Yeah, baby, about freakin' time!" Fuka-ziroh exclaimed, all of her anger forgotten and replaced with excitement. As a gamer, this was the kind of stuff that seemed likely to appeal to her—and appeal it did.

"Let's check it out before we move. Everyone, together," M commanded, bringing the group closer. Every other surviving team would be watching their devices for the rules, so the likelihood of being attacked was almost nil.

"All right, kids! Everyone line up here!" Pitohui called out, waving her gun around. The KTR-09 with its seventy-five-round drum magazine must have been quite heavy, but she waved it about as lightly as if it were a flag.

Llenn quickly darted over to the hollow in the ground where Pitohui was located and slid into it on her tush. One of the benefits of grassland was the extra momentum one could get when sliding. Next came Fukaziroh, with an MGL-140 in each hand, and lastly M, with his M14 EBR.

The hollow space was about five yards across. The four of them faced one another and waited out the last ten seconds.

Breeep!

The ugly alarm went off again, lighting up their device screens.

Whatever this special rule is, I just want to fight SHINC, Llenn repeated to herself, waiting for the text to pop up on the terminal in her hands. She wasn't particularly worried. It wasn't like they were going to say *Stop fighting right now, and whoever makes friends with everyone else first wins!* Squad Jam was, from start to finish, a virtual bloodbath, one that would last until there was only one team remaining.

"Special rule announcement and activation."

There was the text. It scrolled automatically from bottom to top. There was also a scroll bar on the right edge to go back and reread the message.

Okay, what's it gonna be? Llenn wondered, following the moving text.

"At the end of this message, one person will be designated from each surviving team."

All right, so one person will be picked by the staff. I suppose that the special rule will apply to that person, she thought, reading on. The message was nice and slow and clear, to ensure it was properly understood.

"The designation will be spelled out on the terminal of the chosen player."

That's why they were supposed to stop and watch their devices. No fear of the message getting lost.

"The designation is not by random, but chosen for the purposes of game balance by the staff and sponsor observing the event."

Well, if they're going to implement this special rule, they might as well make sure it plays out ideally and doesn't get wasted because of a fluke random draw. And if balance is important, that would be why they gave themselves some breathing room by stating the range of "six to eight teams."

"Victory conditions will be altered for the chosen players."

Hmm? How so?

"The chosen players will leave their teams as betrayers. The betrayers will form a new team that will fight together from this point onward."

What?! Llenn thought, right as Fukaziroh exclaimed, "Whoo!"

"For a period of time, all weapons will be locked. Transportation will be provided to send the betrayers to convene with the rest of their team, opening up travel to the UNKNOWN *area."*

Huh? Wha—? Why? Hwah? Um? Wait? What?

Llenn's mind was mostly stuck.

"Ooooh! Llenn, I've never seen you make that stupid of a face! Damn, wish I could take a picture!" raved Fukaziroh from her left.

"I see. So that's why they set up that central area and submerged the island. The teams left over have no choice but to go there," M observed calmly.

Llenn recovered enough of her wits to speak again. "Hey! Wait a second! This is messed up! What about the team?! What about our inseparable bond of friendship?!" she lamented, punctuation flying.

"But rules are rules. They're meant to be followed," Fukaziroh replied.

It was absolutely the most serious expression Llenn had ever seen Fukaziroh make. *Damn, wish I could take a picture.*

"Now go forth and kill. Your former comrades are now your enemies," the message continued, as it scrolled upward.

And then, seconds later, just over the top of her own Satellite Scan terminal, Llenn saw a wicked smile on Pitohui's face.

"Whoo-hoo! Yeah! It's meeee! Now I get to fight Llenn!"

"Pardon?"

To be continued...

SPECIAL TEARJERKER EPIC III
I Fight With My Pride on the Line!
~I Write, Therefore I Fight! Let the Soul of My Gunshot Tentatively Roar~

He was struggling.

How do I stand out? How do I become celebrated? How do I get seen as a champion?

In short, he wanted to be a hero who everyone looked up to—in Squad Jam.

At this point, you can probably tell who *he* is.

It was none other than the middle-aged author who set up the first Squad Jam and got bashed when he sent out autographed copies of his own books to the winners. He seemed to think that just because he knew a few things about guns, he was therefore the best writer of gunfights in the entire world.

A generous fan might assume that it meant he would be good at shooting, too, but that could not be further from the truth. He was restless and hated practicing in general, so the best you could say about his skill was that he was as bad at shooting as he was obsessed with it.

Once he successfully launched his sponsorship of the first Squad Jam, he managed to take part using his own avatar without anyone realizing it, but SHINC easily destroyed him in unceremonious fashion.

In SJ2, he was beat to the sponsoring punch by Pitohui, so he entered the tournament himself, swearing revenge (in multiple ways), but an early skirmish left him injured and missing his weapon.

He vowed to die in a blaze of glory, so he leaped into the fray with a grenade in his hand, only to find that no enemies were around anymore. Therefore, he blew himself up while feeling relieved, about as dumb an ending as anyone could envision, and it drew more than a few stifled chuckles from the audience.

Argh, it's so frustrating! I want to show off more! I know I can! he thought, full of resentment and anger. The only thing that could bring an end to that frustration would be to sponsor SJ3 before anyone else could.

So he sent Zaskar, the company that ran *GGO*, an obnoxiously long e-mail, until they finally sent back a response that said *Fine, we'll do it, just stop sending us these stalker-ish messages.*

He was also annoyingly insistent with his suggestion of a special rule, which they played along with. He even got a little encouragement: "Whatever, just do what you want."

He reached out to his *GGO* friends, all of whom put up with his unfortunate personality, and he recruited a few new companions to assemble a team for SJ3. This time, he made sure he was ready. He abandoned his actual job in order to put all of his time into *GGO*, beefing up his avatar. He might have had a middle-aged gut in real life, but in the game, he was a macho tough guy.

His main weapon was still the SG 550 sniper rifle that he bought with real currency, but to make sure he was completely outfitted for battle, he acquired an MP5SD3 silenced submachine gun, the SIG P226 pistol, and the

Benelli M3 shotgun. He was armed to the teeth like a damn fool.

And no, he didn't put any of them into his inventory until they were needed. He kept each and every gun out on his person, a true man's man ready for anything battle could throw at him. A damn fool, indeed.

Then the preliminary round arrived.

It was time for him to be a man. He might have been a chicken in real life, but at least in *GGO*, he was a fearless warrior. He was known as "virtual Benkei," after the famous warrior monk who wore all of his weapons on his back into battle. Better than being a chicken, right?

Because the arena of the prelim round was long and narrow, there was no need to worry about running or hiding. It was all-out attack time.

"Let's go, boys!" the author shouted, all bravery now. This round would be a brief, single opportunity to advance. The crude method of overwhelming the enemy with firepower was also an effective one. His companions followed behind him.

And there was the enemy, visible behind a distant barricade. They were aware of their opponent, too, but they hadn't expected such a reckless charge and weren't ready to return fire yet. This was his big chance. Time to capitalize.

"Heh-heh-heh! The time has come for my fangs to howl! My soul quakes with midnight!" he shouted, attempting to sound cool but mixing his metaphors something fierce. He stopped in his tracks and raised the SG 550 to blast the enemy.

"Hubh!" "Hrng!" "Bwah!" "Guoh!"

His companions around him made an assortment of silly noises as they got shot. Their bodies glowed with gunshot effects, and they collapsed. Forward.

"Ga-whuh?" the author gasped. Where in the world had *that* noise come from? His eyes bulged in disbelief at the sight of his teammates dying.

And he couldn't be blamed. They'd all been shot in the back.

"Ha!"

The author spun around. He saw the gun muzzle pointed toward him and the bullet line emerging from it.

Barely thirty feet away, his hundred-round M4A1 assault rifle pointed at the fallen teammates, was the man who'd signed up for the team just the other day. He never took his sunglasses off, and his name was Kadowaka. His skill and stats were good, and he seemed quite comfortable playing VR games. He'd been a promising member of the team, until…

"Have you gone mad?! How dare you shoot the comrades who were supposed to make me look good!" the author screamed, forehead veins bulging.

Kadowaka replied, "Sorry, but you're going to die here, too. You won't be appearing in the SJ3 final." His expression was unreadable behind the sunglasses, but his voice was clear and cold.

"Wha—?! What did you say?!"

"You forget your job as a writer, wasting your time with games. Deplorable. Your deadline is in three days. Go back to the real world."

"Wha—?! How do you know about my deadline…?" The author's face swiftly changed from fury to terror. "N-no… It can't be… You're the man who sends writers and illustrators obsessed with VR games back to reality—"

Ba-ba-ba-ba-ba-ba-ba-ba-ba-bakk!

The M4A1 rattled.

"Guhhh…"

The author slumped to the ground, full of holes like Swiss cheese.

Lastly, Kadowaka pulled out a four-inch barrel S&W Model 19 revolver and pressed the end to his own temple.

"Didn't my name tip you off? In fact, I made it extra obvious..."

Blam.

He killed off his own avatar.

"The Kadokawa editorial office hires an incredible VR assassin to do their dirty work..."

The urban legend turned out to be true. When the word got out among the gamer authors and illustrators, the creative types banded together to form a counterplan, kicking off a new round of the eternal battle between artists and editors...but that is a story for another day.

The End

Llenn appears as a support character in the game *Dengeki Bunko Fighting Climax Ignition* for PS4, PS3, and PS Vita, only in Japan.

(You can look up the details on the official site.)

Kino from *Kino's Journey* is also a support character in the game, so you can experience the dream confrontation of Llenn vs. Kino.

If you want to see Llenn moving and talking, check it out!

I play with Kuroko Shirai using Llenn as a support.

Here is Karen Kohiruimaki struggling with the input device of the old-school retro hardware.

This has been Kouhaku Kuroboshi.